TWISTED

lola smirnova

TWISTED

lola smirnova

Quickfox
publishing

Published by Quickfox Publishing

PO Box 12028 Mill Street 8010

Cape Town, South Africa

www.quickfox.co.za | info@quickfox.co.za

First edition 2014

TWISTED

ISBN 978-1-496-03101-3

Edited by Angela Voges and Chuck S.

Proofread by Vanessa Wilson

Front cover photography by Bradley Ruiters

DISCLAIMER

All names and characters appearing in this work are fictitious.
Any resemblance to real persons, living or dead, is purely
coincidental.

Thank you Chuck S.
for making the right turn.
Without you this book
would not be possible.
Love you…

1

'*Sag es!*' he screams at me.

The heavy motorcycle helmet is so tightly strapped to my head that I can hear the blood rushing through my ears. The smell of stale sweat reeks from the worn padding inside it. I struggle to swallow. A drop of spit runs down the ball gag that has been shoved into my mouth, then down my chin, and drips onto the couch beneath my knees. My shoulders are screaming from the pull of the handcuffs, which force my hands together behind my back.

He stands in the middle of the small and gloomy room and I can see the outline of his large body. Two bloodshot eyes are firmly fixed on my exposed nipples.

A fleshy tongue slides backwards and forwards through the gap in his teeth. He licks the sweat off his lips, moans, and starts rubbing his groin, rocking his wide hips back and forth. He increases the pace, while his moans get louder and louder. Next, he stops abruptly, moving his eyes from my chest to my face, scowls, and takes a few menacing steps towards me. I shrink instinctively, tensing my body …

'I know him. Don't be scared Jul. He's a bit strange, but a harmless motherfucker.' That is what my sister, Natalia, managed to whisper in my ear half an hour ago, before I followed this freak, with the brain bucket in his hand, upstairs.

Natalia and I were sitting at the bar counter when he walked in. He didn't even have a drink; just stepped in the door, looked around, stopped his stare at me, and mumbled, 'I want *you*. Let's go.'

'It's time to work!' teased Natalia. Her naughty look followed us all the way up the stairs.

'*Sag es!*' the crack-head screams again, which I think means 'say it' in Luxembourgish or German.

He grunts, and with a wild thrust shoves his hips right into my face. He doesn't even bother to take his jeans off. A quick unzip and he pulls out a flaccid penis, puts one foot up on the couch and starts violently pumping it, so close that his clenched palm is punching the helmet. Lucky for me the visor is shut.

I sigh deeply and try to shift on the couch to get rid of the cramps, which start crawling up my legs and back.

A bit strange? Come on, Natalia! You could call him anything – cracked, insane, alien on Earth – but hardly 'a bit strange'!

I glance at the half-empty bottle of champagne seductively chilling in the ice bucket. If I'd known what Natalia had meant by 'a bit strange', I would have finished it before he handcuffed me and shoved the damn ball into my jaws.

'Sag es!' brings me out of my thoughts again.

I peep at his red face … What the hell does this crack-head think he is doing? I wouldn't even call it masturbation! He tortures his penis in a spasmodic exertion. The awful tongue tossing in his distorted mouth, the dark brown hair stuck to the film of sweat on his broad brow, and the whimpering noises coming out of his fat body make a disgusting spectacle.

'Sag es!'

According to the instructions he gave me before we started this session, I was supposed to say 'I love you, I forgive you' through the gag.

I wonder what my seventh-grade teacher would say if she walked in the door right now? She always believed in me and encouraged: 'You are going to come out on top,

Julia …' Good shot, Anna Ivanovna. You were pretty close!

He shuts his eyes and wrinkles his forehead in concentration. Frustrated, he drops his limp penis and squats next to the small table in the centre of the room. He pauses only to wipe the trickle of sweat from his forehead. Then he quickly snorts the line of blow on the glass table, and doesn't get up for a while, staring deadpan at the wall.

Hey, fat boy, get on with it so we can have some together after this. I think I deserve a little pick-me-up for my efforts here.

I wonder what could possibly have happened to turn his grey matter inside out like this. A few hours later, when I kick my 'labour hour' around with the girls, they will tell me some rumours about him having had a motorbike accident. Apparently, he was riding 'under the influence' with his fiancée in tow. She died there on the street, in his arms, in a puddle of mud. With the last beats of her heart, he stared at her wide-open eyes, full of terror, and at her bleeding lips that breathed in agony: 'Please, baby, I don't want to die.'

I shudder. I don't know if he was injured in the accident, but after this short time we've spent together I can assure you that his brain was nowhere to be found after that crash.

'Sag es!'

Yeah, whatever …

He finally comes back to the couch, pulling and beating his poor half-dead cock in front of my plastic shield. I try to say what he demands – anything to get this over and done with, and me out of here – but 'I love you', that forms beautifully in my throat, dissolves into an incoherent mumble as it hits the ball.

His small eyes devour every inch of my naked body, which is truly just skin and bone with boyish nipples where there are supposed to be breasts. The only reason why any man would choose to fuck me (aside from being a paedophile, of course) would be my big blue eyes and long blonde hair.

'*Sag es!*'

His whole face is scrunched up in an ugly leer and his bottom lip is quivering as he makes a weird whining noise.

Oh please! Don't tell me you are going to cry now! Pathetic, sick, even disturbing, but not just 'a bit strange', Natalia?!

He keeps on yanking and jerking and thrusting like a maniac – harder and harder. He's going to pull that thing off if he doesn't stop!

'*Sag es! Sag es!*' he whines over and over, then forcefully flips the visor up and pulls the bottom of the helmet so close that his soft crotch hits my face. I shut my eyes a second before the first squirt of semen hits them.

'It's over' slips with warmth and ease into my head, then streams down through my body, echoing the semen on my face. My eyes are closed but I can still hear him sobbing, sniffling and mumbling.

I can't believe this fucker just ruined my make-up!

All I've got from this pathetic episode is an experience I will never be able to share with my grandchildren and €60 with no promise of a tip.

2

My name is Julia. I am from Ukraine. I work as an
entertainer in one of the many cabarets in Luxembourg
City. In other words … I am a prostitute.

Luxembourg City is the capital of the Grand Duchy
of Luxembourg, the pint-sized, landlocked country in
the heart of Western Europe. By Shanghai, London
or New York's standards, it wouldn't be strange to
have sixty champagne bars in one city, but it does
sound quirky when you consider that Luxembourg
City is twice as small as Orlando Disney World.

This sleepy and conservative locale, the world's
eighth-largest banking and financial centre, mother-
land of prioress Yolanda and the 100-watt radio

transmitter, is stuffed with sex-orientated 'establishments', like the one where I work. What's more,
they are jam-packed with able-to-eat-a-horse-for-
the-dough girls from different countries – mostly, of
course, Eastern Europeans, who would do anything
to make an extra buck.

Champagne bar, whorehouse, brothel, house
of assignation, bordello, den of vice; call them
what you like, it does not change the core of these
places. Although they are often called cabarets, and
occasionally there is even strip-dancing involved,
you shouldn't associate them with merrymaking or
extravaganza. 'Trade', 'sex', 'transactions', 'carnal',
'barter' or 'perversion' would be the better words to
portray this type of nightery.

This is a place where one man can spend
thousands of euro in an hour or sip only Coke all
night long; where the currency is not money but
champagne; where often nobody is really interested
in the champagne's quality or taste, but rather finds
its value in the size and quantity of the bottles; where
the sanctity of the sparkling drink of the gods and the
missionary position are lost in the blue confusion of
fake orgasms and sex noises.

It works as simply as a jukebox – to get music, you
have to stick in a coin. If you want a girl to lavish
attention on you, pay for her champagne.

The cheapest option is a €25 glass of bubbly,
which gives you 15 minutes of an affectionate and

solicitous bond with a girl at the bar. Pay twice
that price and your 'date' drinks *piccolo*, the 250 ml
bottle. In this case, the time you spend with her is
doubled, but the storyline stays the same. Next: the
demi-bouteille, a 375 ml bottle that costs about €180
for half an hour. This 'denomination' grants a little
bit of comfort, because both of you can move to a
dim semi-private lounge, as well as the confidence
that physical manipulation will be involved. And
last, but not least, is the 'full house' for the standard
bottle, the price for which varies. It kicks off at €250
for questionable swill, which is reasonable damage
considering that in addition to a drink, you get
screwed for an hour in the *séparé* – a private room,
most commonly upstairs. You could be asked to pay
up to €650 for Cristal or Dom Perignon, where, of
course, you cough up not only for sex but also for the
champagne's snobbish name, fine finish in the mouth,
and the supplementary fondness and devotion. Sad
to say, these pricey bottles – and the one-and-a-half
litre magnums that go for €1,000 or more – are a rare
occurrence in these clubs.

The uniqueness of such places is that while you, the
customer, are having leisure time with your 'pick', her
mind is constantly dividing the amount that you've
already spent by five (this is how much commission
the house pays her), adding her €60 daily salary and
planning how to badger you to buy another bottle, all
the while smiling or laughing hard enough to make

sure that all of these calculations in her head are not reflected on her pretty face.

Most of the clubs open at one in the afternoon and cease their trading at about four in the morning. Of course, the run has to be split – there are day and night shifts. Even though, practically, there is no big difference between the two spells, the contrast in the clientele is huge.

The day shift – *fuck, I hate it!* – is all about the married and the perverts, but more often the married perverts. As a rule, they drop by to use their lunch break for a dull, uncomplicated quickie, or for depraved 'activities' they have never had the guts to share with their wives and girlfriends. They don't drink much and have limited time. That is why the club is usually boring and full of freaks, but in the end, who cares if you can get the bottle?

On the other hand, the night transforms the club and fills it with a party flavour – the music is louder, the customers are drunker and the laughter gets more sincere. Even the girls' sweat looks like a piece of cake. The problem is that the boys often get carried away by the alcohol and the thundering crowd, so their brains switch out of sex mode. If there is no sex, there is probably going to be no bottle either.

But enough, I don't want to bore you. Let's set in motion my adventure that, by the way, began without me.

3

One year before the helmet guy, my sisters, Natalia and Lena, decided to go to Luxembourg to make some extra bucks. Irina, their best friend, had gone there before. When she returned, she kept on boasting about big money she had earned there. Moreover, after just a few days of being back at home – in gloomy Kherson, our small town in the south of Ukraine – Irina looked around, crinkled her nose, and fancifully decided to throw a grand in US dollars at a trip to Istanbul, simply because she wanted to hang out with Natalia, who, by that time, had already been living in the big smoke for five years.

Back in the nineties, I wasn't the only one in newly independent, barefoot-but-proud Ukraine, who felt a nasty bitterness about Irina's blow. It didn't matter what occupation or job you had – doctor, teacher, scientist or student – all ex-Soviet folk struggled equally, seldom able to stretch their money further than the rice or potatoes on their plates.

Funny, when Natalia asked what kind of job it was, Irina, with an innocence in her voice that didn't match the hussy look in her eyes, just prattled, 'Dancing in a nightclub.'

'Whatever! For that cash I would eat from the dirty floor!' flashed through Natalia's mind. She was fed up with trying to make a living by doing a 'proper' job. Therefore, it was a perfect moment for Irina to plant seeds of doubt in my sister's soaked-up-in-suppressed-depression head…

Well, imagine our shock when, a few months before the end of Natalia's final grade and the school exams, she decided to drop out and take off. She wanted to escape from run-down Ukraine with no hope for its future – where the best-case scenario would be her selling goods from Turkey or China on the free market – and run to unknown Istanbul, with no guarantee that she would even get a job but with the faith that somewhere there, if she worked hard and used any opportunity, a better life would be waiting for her.

When Mom found out about Natalia's big plans, she took her for a long walk. A few hours later, at a family meeting, standing in front of us in the middle of the living room, she announced, 'It definitely is an avant-garde decision, but I am inclined to support Natalia's choice.'

My sister cried out, '*Da!*'

Our father became furious and started yelling 'Mad women!' and then 'I can't fight all four of you!' Luckily, our mother knew how to handle him. She added, 'Yuri, our girl is determined to start an adult life with or without us, so I suggest we do anything to make it with us.'

He stopped arguing, but stayed hellishly mad. Of course, eventually, our father found peace, together with the principal of one of the local schools, who agreed to issue a school-leaving certificate for a straight-A student for only fifty US bucks – with Natalia's name on it.

Natalia moved with Mom to Istanbul. Even though my sister never regretted her decision – she went overseas, lived in a big city and had a real adult life with real adult dreams – it wasn't a summer camp for her either.

By that time, Mom was holding Russian language courses for Turkish entrepreneurs in small and medium-sized businesses. They sold their goods – leather, textiles, clothes and shoes – to traders from Russia and Ukraine. She managed to find a job for

Natalia, making tea and coffee in some shipping company, which ran from a huge and sophisticated office, with a long set of wall-sized windows overlooking the Bosphorus. My sister got the best deal, that's for sure, considering she didn't speak Turkish and had no work experience. Her big, dark eyes, her childishly cute but at the same time intricate face, and mop of curly burnt-umber hair, together with her slightly heavy hips, which were balanced by bursting-at-the-seams boobs on a tight body, got her her first job, paying $300 per month.

During these years, Natalia mastered the Turkish language and used any opportunity to get the hang of all types of office work, including how to manage the re-supply of cargo ships. She even learnt about shipping brokerage. She had also got herself involved in a tiring, full-of-empty-promises relationship with her boss. The fucker was married with two kids, and was almost twenty years older than her. He loved to impress Natalia with a good dinner at a fancy restaurant and clumsy sex for dessert in the apartment he rented for such occasions. He generously shared endless wisdom about life with her, as well as gifts of cheap jewellery that he presented to her as if they were diamonds.

He also had a truly Turkish way of becoming over-suspicious from time to time. Natalia would get into trouble if one of the restaurant's other male patrons looked at her, for whatever reason: either some man would find her pretty, or, as often happens in restaurants, someone would get bored and just look around at others. Once, he even got pissed off when she asked a male waiter for directions to the bathroom, causing a scene in front of everybody that ended with him slapping her sharply in the face.

The jealousy of this man was often caused by absolute absurdity, as was the case with his own business partner, who was a Russian ex-captain. The Russian was practically Natalia's boss too, but because he was a handsome man and famous for his Casanova reputation, he often caused my sister's boss-lover to yell at her during his moments of groundless rage – which usually ended up with him calling her a Russian whore who was no different from the other prostitutes who overran the city.

The bastard would be satisfied and stop his ugly, jealous scenes only once he'd brought her to tears. At the same time he constantly fed her bullshit about how unhappy he was with his wife and that the only reason he didn't end the nightmare of his marriage was because of his kids: 'The divorce would devastate them,' he always said with great concern on his face.

No shit! Devastating my sister, instead, was the perfect solution, then?

So, her life was quite intense: ten-hour workdays often without lunch breaks and days off; hours spent on public transport in the city's heavy, endless traffic; wasted tears and ragged nerves from the love story with the boss. Hers was a life of haste and too little sleep, chronic fatigue, and eyes that were red and swollen from crying.

Don't get me wrong – Natalia was not a hard-labour victim. Her life involved absolutely normal things that many people have to do in order to survive. But I do want to make a point: her future decision was not the result of failure or laziness.

By the end of her fifth year of climbing the career ladder, desperately trying to improve her life and the living conditions of our family, she had got by earning $1,000 and the privilege of having a lunch break. Of course, a great salary if she was staying in La Paz, Bolivia, or even in our Kherson. In Istanbul it was not a living, but simply holding on to life. Eventually, she lost her faith in the possibility of having a decent income. The frequent nightmares started, in which she'd wake up in 20 years' time in the same office, at the same computer, earning only $500 more, and having finally got a legitimate place in her boss's family – as wife number three or four.

4

The trip to Luxembourg could have been a perfect chance for Lena, my middle sister, to change her life too. She was always tangled in endless-love-forever stories with all kinds of losers.

It would be easier for you to understand Lena's problem if you could meet her in person. Tall and beautiful, she resembled Drew Barrymore, but with chestnut hair. Her body was fit and flawless, especially since becoming a student of the Kherson Cultural College's choreography department. She had an extremely soft and friendly nature; she simply never learnt how to say no. This, with her looks, drew men – mostly jerks – like the light draws moths.

She constantly dwelled in a fairyland. The only thing she wanted was marriage and a bunch of kids. What's more, she was convinced that this was the only way she could ever be happy.

I always wondered when we 'lost' her. Was it as early as when we watched Cinderella animations, or later, while she was reading *Scarlet Sails* by Alexander Grin? We were raised on the same books and movies. Why was it different with her? I guess during one of those screened tearjerkers she felt so comfortable and secure in the fantasy that she decided never to come back to Earth.

All of Lena's life was built on this one dream ...

The first serious relationship she had was when she was in the eighth grade. His name was Serega. Sad, but after that 'love story' I will never be able to associate this name with anything rosy. He was in his last year of school, three years older than her, involved with the local youth gang whose members were familiar with stealing, drugs, and who knew what else. We all knew Serega was a bastard, but Lena wouldn't listen ...

I'm telling you, totally in fairyland...

Two years of happily ever after ended with an ugly incident that put me in hospital, caused tons of pain and tears, and Lena's self-reproach for her unforeseen and non-participative bit in that 'anti-social behaviour'. Afterwards, unintentionally, I learned how to use her guilt-ridden feelings towards me to my advantage.

Then, there was this Slavic fellow. They met when she was already a college student. Lena truly thought he was the one, and that they would spend the rest of their lives together. Apparently, they didn't think alike. He was an excellent storyteller. One day, after a whole year of sharing an 'unbelievably strong' connection, he disappeared. Then she received the coward's letter: 'Sorry baby, but I've been lying to you all this time – I have a wife and two kids. Forgive me'. The comeback from this fairyland was as messy as the previous one. Lena tried to kill herself. Luckily, her knowledge of how to cut vital veins was second-rate; the only outcomes Lena achieved were scaring the shit out of us and spoiled wallpaper in the bedroom, which still has dark and awful stains on it.

By the time the trip came up, Lena was in the middle of another drama. I remember that night as if it were today. We were drinking cheap, sweet wine and smoking long and trendy cigarettes on the balcony of our apartment. My sister was sobbing, and smearing the snot and mascara over her face – 'I can't believe he wants me to do this! I can't believe he wants this!'

By 'this' she meant an abortion.

In short: they had been together for almost two years, and were often too lazy to use a rubber. She'd got pregnant. While she was picking a name for the baby, the husband-to-be confessed that he wasn't ready for it yet.

I sipped my wine, drew on my cigarette, and sighed deeply. For a second, I wondered how we could accommodate the prospective baby, considering that the father still lived on campus while Lena and I shared a bedroom in our parents' small apartment.

I nodded and agreed with Lena's affirmation of him being a total bastard, but at the same time, praised the fella in my head. I thought that if it wasn't for him getting cold feet, my crazy sister would definitely keep the baby, and probably mess up her life even more. Come on! Even at seventeen, I knew that babies are a very cute but extremely expensive 'hobby' to have. Food, living space, nappies, doctors, medicines, clothes, school fees, you name it!

In the middle of our little gathering Lena's cellphone rang. It was Natalia. She quickly wiped her face and cleared her throat, trying to sound casual. Then, 'Hi, Nata!'

I sighed again, and thought that life was so unfair. Lena never turned on the waterworks in front of Natalia. With me, she could go for hours. The fact that Lena used me as her tissue all the time started irritating me.

'Are you crying again?' I heard Natalia's muffled voice in Lena's brick. I smiled – she knew her sister too well to be fooled.

'Len, stop moaning, let's get our visas to Luxembourg and fuck off. You need a break; I desperately need some changes, too.'

Lena snivelled, 'Are you sure we can trust Irina? I don't want to get into one of those scary stories about girls being enslaved. They talk about them on TV all the time!'

The voice in the receiver quivered, 'Fuck Irina and your scary stories! I called the embassy and checked – it's all legitimate, so the risks are considerably low.'

'Well, I don't know ...' Lena moaned after a pause.

'Come on, sister!' Natalia almost squealed. 'I know it's scary, but trust me, it will be fine. You know I need you on this one! I swear that if you say no, I'll kill myself and leave a note: For everything I blame my indecisive sister Lena.'

We burst into extended belly laughter, ending up with tears in our eyes.

The decision was made!

5

Before my sisters took off, Lena had an abortion and Natalia quit her job in Istanbul. During the trip, they called almost every week and reported that they were fine. In the meantime, I was in my last year of school, trying my best to combine my soaked in booze and weed nightlife with school and my damn homework. I still managed to get fairish marks and – more importantly – not to get pregnant.

One evening, a few weeks before my sisters were due to return, my father and I were having dinner at home. It was a typical supper of borsch, a traditional Ukrainian beetroot soup, and potatoes fried in lard with chopped onions. As always, our conversation hardly went further than, 'How was school?' or 'Have you done your homework?'

Then, out of the blue, my father turned his attentive look to me, narrowed his eyes and said, 'Don't even think about it!'

Hmm … all I had in mind was how to sponge a few *hryvni*[1] for tomorrow's night out, so I just raised my eyebrows in return.

'Don't even think about going with your sisters!' he snarled. 'Jul, you are too smart for this. Remember, when you were a little girl, you always wanted to be a doctor?'

Unintentionally I rolled my eyes.

'Don't pull your faces here, in front of me!' he raised his voice.

'Pa, please …' I begged wearily.

Un-fucking-fortunately, the supper had gone from casual to seriously annoying.

'Don't "pa" at me! You need to have a degree to become something in this life or to find a good job.'

I flew into a rage. 'Where is your diploma, Pa, huh? How is your degree helping you now? It's been almost six months since they laid you off and you are still jobless!' I uttered and ran out of the kitchen.

The saddest part was that not only my father was canned; the whole post-Soviet belt was in the same jam, too.

---

1 Natural currency of Ukraine since 2 September 1996

Let's take the Kherson shipbuilding yard, where my father worked for almost twenty years. In 1991 it closed down and thousands of people, like him, lost their jobs. What's more, the teachers, doctors, policemen, soldiers, pensioners – anyone who depended on government – didn't get their salaries for months, even years. So, the educators' hunger strikes or medics' refusal to come to work, ignoring the Hippocratic oath in a desperate fight for their shamefully low salaries, were normal, everyday events.

The mere idea of going to the university for at least five years and becoming, let's say, a doctor, and then getting a place in a local hospital with a salary of $120 per month made me nauseous.

The only people who had a halfway decent life those days (except for the greedy, corrupt politicians, other officials, gang members, or the blessed ones who were lucky in some way to be close to the trough) were the ones who didn't look back, left behind their ideas of a cloyingly planned and secure Soviet past, and adapted to a new life full of risks and surprises. Among them were suitcase traders who knocked about in Poland and Turkey; sailors who managed to find jobs on foreign ships; men who did rock-fall reconstructions in Portugal or harvested crops in Spain; older women who usually looked after the elderly in Europe, Canada or the United States; and the younger ones, like me and my sisters, who took care of more-capable-of-action clients in the 'entertainment' business.

The memories of a three-litre glass jar full of evenly cut squares of pork fat, preserved in thick layers of coarse salt, with skin that was impossible to chew, will stay with me forever. This was often the only item in our fridge for months. The image of our mother's constantly worried eyes, the shame on our father's face each time he came back home with the same nothing as the day before, will never be erased from my head.

Even when they found a few *hryvni* to buy 500 grams of rice and some bread for that day, or the rare occasion when one of our mom's friends who worked at the kindergarten helped by bringing some scraps that even the not-so-picky staff would not take home, the misery wouldn't disappear – the question of what to feed to their three children tomorrow still hung densely in the air.

Eventually, our mother didn't have a choice but to go abroad to work. Thanks to her fearless and adventurous character, and later to Natalia's great desire to swim out of that hopeless and depressing puddle called life in post-Soviet Ukraine, my unemployed father and I could afford borsch and some fruit for dessert that evening.

In addition to finding a job and making some money to help us to avoid complete deprivation, our mom also taught us to be brave and always to look for a way out – even if you could not see one.

So yes, instead of discouraging me, my father unwillingly nudged me to the realization that no matter what, I had to leave Kherson. There was no other way for me. The only thing I had to do was to announce it to my sisters. Something was telling me that it could be a bump in the road.

6

Lena and Natalia had been back in Kherson for four months when I decided, finally, to take action and talk to them. It was my birthday, too, which was a part of my strategy for persuading them to take me on their next trip.

Oh yes, of course there was going to be another trip.

They'd spent half the year in Luxembourg and managed to earn an astronomical amount: about $20,000 each! But because their income was the only source of finance for our family, and my sisters were, to some extent, hooked on shopping and partying, the liquid assets evaporated pretty quickly.

They decided to go back.

Unfortunately, they had to wait another two months. According to Luxembourgish immigration law, entertainers were not allowed to work and stay in the country for more than six consecutive months. They also had to have a break between trips, out of Luxembourg, that had to be as long as the time they'd spent there. Fortunately for me, this meant that I still had time to finish my school exams.

I knew there was going to be a problem. Both sisters had always been overprotective of me. They wanted to make sure that I had the best opportunities – me becoming a hooker was obviously not one of them.

Natalia, as the eldest sister, had a persistent urge to stick up for me. Lena was driven by the guilt I mentioned earlier. I could get whatever I wanted from my kin by manipulating their feelings – *I know I am a spoilt bitch* – but this time my advantage actually played against me.

We had finished the cake, and our father had left the three of us in the kitchen for his quiet moment with the TV and the beloved ten-year-old couch.

It was a really special night – Baileys and cigars. Natalia had generously forked out to celebrate my eighteenth birthday. The sweet liquor made us pretty tipsy, and our chat more upfront and revealing. The girls went on about the memories of their trip.

'We were scared shitless when the airplane touched down at Luxembourg International. It was night-time too...' Natalia sipped from her glass and continued, 'Max, our talent agent, picked us up. He was suspiciously quiet and uneasy. The five kilometre drive to the club felt like the longest trip ever. No wonder he gave us goose bumps: a few weeks later we found out that he was a total junkie.'

'He was supposed to get us a contract at another club for the next month,' Lena jumped in, 'and also to renew the visas, which had to be done every month. Guess what – this fucker disappeared! We didn't know what to do. Luckily, we managed to find another agent to sort it out. But still, it was a troubling story for us and for Max, too. After all, he was found dead in his apartment from an overdose. Apparently the guy didn't have family, because they started looking for him only when the stink of his body reeked through the walls.'

'That's another story, Len. Stop interrupting me!' Natalia exclaimed with childish excitement. She'd won back a turn to speak. 'When Max pulled up in the middle of the narrow and murky street, right next to the lone, dowdy neon sign – "Platinum Triangle" – I thought we were in the middle of some horror movie!'

'I promise you Jul,' Lena broke in again. 'The letter P was flickering on and off while sending off sparks!'

'It was nothing like we imagined it would be. You know, we had this Las Vegas-type of place in mind.' We burst into laughter.

They entered the dark and smoky place, which had a long passage with a bar that stretched along the right and sank into a big square lounge with low couches, red curtains and a small stage in the corner. An old, awfully tall lady with a gloomy face behind the counter looked at them and solemnly nodded at Max, who was pulling their luggage in and missed the 'mafia move'.

The place looked weird. It had about twenty dressed-up, heavily painted girls: a few of them moved lazily on the stage; the tipsy one at the bar was persistently soft-soaping the only customer, who had a terrorised look on his face; and the rest were sitting on the row of stools all the way along the left side of the corridor, which looked really funny opposite the elevated bar.

When my sisters stepped inside, all the girls (even the drunk one) turned to look at them in the hope of seeing more clients at the door. As soon as they recognised Max and figured that my sisters were the new dancers, the expressions on their faces changed to 'Fuck! We can't believe this old, giant bitch is featherbedding, when the club is empty every night!' Their last hopes of making some money in that shithole evaporated on the arrival of those two.

The giant bitch was Rosy, the owner of the club. She stepped out from behind the counter and, without saying hello to the new arrivals, called one of the girls.

'Show them around', said Rosy, levelling a distinct misanthropy at the pretty blonde she'd called, before going back to the bar.

The excessively friendly and energetic girl reached to shake my sisters' hands. 'Hi, my name is Angel,' she said. After a brief pause, she smiled and added in Russian, 'That's my stage name. My real name is Olga.'

When Max had eventually settled their suitcases and hotfooted it away, Olga took them on the tour, explaining their duties and club's utilities. When they went upstairs to see the private rooms, their bleached usher abruptly turned and said, with a knowing smile on her face, 'You are not allowed to have sex with the customers,' then kept moving onward.

'We both sighed with relief,' Natalia carried on, as Lena nodded.

Suddenly father walked into the kitchen. We fell silent, exchanging glances on our blushing faces: we had never spoken to him about what my sisters did and always tried to keep our voices low to make sure he would not accidently hear us. Clearly, the reality in which Natalia and Lena had being working as pros was 'slightly' changed to a version in which they were waitressing.

It was common for working girls to lie to their families. How could one tell her mom that she was nothing but a whore? Of course she would come up with a more palatable interpretation – that she was working as a babysitter or a cleaning lady. And even though the money she earned was freaking huge for such a short period, and for a four-dollar-an-hour job, her mom, of course, would disregard the obvious and swallow the comfy colouring. How could a mother admit that her girl was nothing but a whore?

'Come on, girls. How many times have I told you not to smoke inside?' Our father went on, bawling us out: 'Go onto the balcony! There is so much smoke in here you can hang an axe in the air!' He pulled his usual disappointed face, opened the window wider, and went back to his beloved.

We cracked up as he left, but decided to move anyway. Natalia grabbed the bottle while Lena and I took the ashtray and the glasses. We parked on the old brown pleather corner seat, which for a typical concrete Soviet-realism-style apartment building was a real luxury. The night was warm and quiet, as it is in the Kherson summer; the shrill chirping of crickets accompanied our straight talk, which we didn't start until we'd made sure that the door behind us was closed.

'So yes,' resumed Natalia, 'the words – no prostitution – were like balm for our exhausted nerves.'

My sisters wanted to believe this fib so badly that they forgot about their conversation with Irina, who had, after all, confessed about what kind of 'dancing' she performed. Moreover, the sign in Russian next to every private room – 'Throw condoms into the crapper only – NEVER INTO A WASTEBIN. Management.' – that was aimed at the girls in case of a police raid, didn't make them think twice.

'Imagine, Jul, our faces, when in the middle of that first night the rhythmical beat of the couch against the wall in the private room next to our accommodation, accompanied by dull pants and sighs – soprano and baritone in unison – woke us.' We rolled with laughter again.

Suddenly I fired it off: 'I am going with you this time.'

They froze for a second and then exclaimed as one, 'No way!'

I started gabbling something about being mature and capable and responsible and I don't remember what else.

'It's a bad idea!' exclaimed Natalia

'It wouldn't be the right place for you, especially not after what you went through three years ago, Jul …' Lena shook her head while looking away.

'What does that have to do with my future plans? I can't believe you brought it up, Len! So now, because you cannot deal with your guilt issues you are going to seal me in a jar and store me in a cool and dry place so I won't get hurt again? Is that your plan, Len? To keep me safe, turning me into a pickled gherkin? It's my life and I will decide what to do with it …'

We argued all night long, until Natalia lost her temper, screamed 'Over my dead body!' and stormed out.

7

Guess what … two months later, three of us are flying to Luxembourg.

Natalia could not stop me, but she did make sure we were going to work in the same place, a cabaret called Sexy Girls.

The hot August day is in full swing when we land. We grab a cab and go straight to the club.

Lena asks the driver to pull off next to the four-storey apartment building with the red sign above the entrance. The billboard with pictures of half-naked girls arrests my attention. Despite the girls' cheesecakes being covered with a glass panel, most of the photos are faded and have curved yellow corners from the merciless sun.

We force our luggage through the doorway and stop in the poky hall. It has a door on the left to the club area, a wall-sized mirror on the right and stairs further down the hall.

While Natalia and Lena are looking for a manager to get the room keys, I avidly peer at the dark bar, taking in every detail. The day shift is rolling. Waves of excitement and fear rage through my body when I think about working here … in just a few hours … tonight!

It's difficult to make out much – after the bright daylight the place looks absolutely pitch-black. All I see is a small group of girls sitting silently on the curved sofa; two men accompanied by sexily dressed girls at the bar, a few steps away from each other; and one sleepy barman. The cigarette smoke and slow, quiet music make them look like a bunch of zombies.

My sisters come back with the keys, and news that there is only one room available with two beds; the others are half-occupied.

It's a real sweat to push the luggage up the narrow, steep stairs, all the way to the fourth floor. The second contains the private rooms, and the third and fourth are the girls' accommodation. As we reach the top, a door on the left flies open. A woman stands at the threshold with a glass of wine in her hand.

'Oh, look who's here! Natalia and her daydreaming sister! Welcome back,' she exclaims in a hoarse and bumbling voice. Then she points at me, discourteously: 'And what is it that you have dragged in with you this time?'

Natalia haplessly sighs, and then greets the woman without even looking at her. 'Hey, Masha.'

She is in her thirties, almost two meters tall, with a strong but beautiful face. Despite the time of the day, Masha is already quite intoxicated. She's wearing a knee-length, pink, slightly wrinkled kimono-like robe, which exposes her athletic legs.

Something tells me Masha used to play basketball … a lot.

Natalia turns to Lena and says quietly, 'You and Jul stay in this room; I will have to share with this one,' and nods towards Masha.

'Wait, wait, wait!' The ball hawk struggles to pronounce the words. 'I don't want you in my room!' She punches the air with the glass of wine and spills some on the decayed linoleum. 'You are crazy with your early jogging! You will wake me up every goddamn morning! I would rather stay with the puny one!' She punches again, this time towards me, and spills more wine.

'What the fuck!' Lena sweeps in. 'She is drunk, Natalia, there's going to be a row.'

I peek into the room, behind Masha's back, who props one side of the doorway up with her shoulder and the other one with her hand. I spot the line of blow on the coffee table, as well as a small plastic bag of grass and an open bottle of wine. 'Why not?' goes through my head, and I say, 'Don't worry, girls, I can stay here. Besides, I do like sleeping late and will be only across the hall from you.' I squeeze in, without even stooping, under Masha's arm. *God, she is a big woman!* I smile to myself, but say only, 'By the way, my name is Julia'.

Masha closes the door, lurches towards the table, drops herself on the couch, temptingly sniffs the line and fills me in: 'My name is Masha, and by the way, I am transsexual.'

8

It has been three weeks since we arrived in Luxembourg and two days since my unforgettable helmet story.

I definitely feel less and less nervous as time goes by, but I am still dealing with some issues – like my childish fear of approaching and talking to strangers; the rejection phobia that is, I think, a common drawback for salespeople of any kind; and taking clients upstairs. After the incident with Lena's Serega I think I will always expect the worst and feel more vulnerable than most. The easiest of the things I had to get used to was taking my clothes off on the stage in front of people.

Who would have thought? Ha!

Of course, I wouldn't be able to handle my new life without the help of alcohol and drugs.

Even though Natalia annoys me by skinning me alive for my regular and heavy consumption, I can never say no to my giant roommate.

Masha has turned out to be a fun girl, as long as she doesn't drink or dope. The booze changes her pretty eyes to mad and inflamed, her muscular but graceful body to rugged and impulsive. As soon as she hits it up, she starts to hate all the girls around her. Yes, she changed her sex, but still doesn't feel complete: unlike the women, she will never be able to reproduce. I guess because my body looks more like it belongs to a ten-year-old boy, jumbo never really disliked me. On the contrary, I am her best buddy now; she shares generously with me.

Masha's hostility is just for appearances. She is mostly harmless. Nevertheless, the girls and many customers try to stay away from her. Once I even witnessed how she staggered, drunk, to a lonely guest who was standing by the bar. The guy was short, with an obedient look; he was sipping an appletini and shuffling on his feet from time to time while wiping the sweat off his bald head. She leaned over him, her dark shadow covering the counter. When he raised his eyes and met with her bull stare, Masha moved closer and slowly whispered 'Heeellooo' in her low voice. The misfit got such a fright that, standing right there, he peed in his pants and ran out of the club, embarrassed …

Shame …!

It is a slow night in the middle of the working week. There is a pair of drunk Portuguese men at the bar. While they are having a drink, another two girls leave with nothing, as the next two draw near to try their luck and convince the men to spend some money on champagne. Natalia and I had our turn earlier and all we could get from them was that in Lisbon they could shag all night for only €50.

You can't beat that, with a minimum here of €250 for an hour.

There are also a few regulars in the club. One goes upstairs straight away with his favourite girl. Another one comes once a week to see Lena. He buys only *demi-bouteilles*, and always tells her that she is a special girl, that he respects her as a woman and will never treat her like a whore by taking her upstairs. In the meantime, the restless hands of this stingy fucker knead and squeeze every spot of her body, while his tongue is constantly deep in her throat, so she can rarely even take a sip from her glass.

The night is quiet and boring, until Natalia's legendary customer, Peter, arrives. As soon as he steps into the club, the barmen and all the girls light up.

The next minute, even the boss and manager are on the floor, dancing the welcome-to-the-best-client-in-the-world dance around him.

It's simple. Peter spends so much money in one night that at his request the boss closes the club for the whole night and all girls entertain only him. The champagne flows without limits. In exchange, he asks for no intimacy of any kind, only participation in his weird fantasy.

Usually, it is a picnic date with Natalia in an imaginary park. Tonight, he wants it to be a rainy summer day. She is his perfect girlfriend and the rest of the girls act like bees, squirrels, flowers or trees. We wear absolutely nothing but some accessories: feelers on springs, plastic animal dominoes, fake flowering twigs.

Even Natalia doesn't know if this is Peter's rolling caprice, or if the guy is totally demented. Who cares, if it's a quick buck and great fun?

When the crazy night is over, at about five in the morning we all end up upstairs in the communal kitchen. We're completely wasted and jolly. The kitchen is fairly clean but well-worn and cluttered, with mostly plastic or aluminum utensils and dishware. We make tea and sandwiches and interrupt one another's yakety-yak, going through the highlights of the night and the other incredible stories and myths about our work.

'I can't believe how much I had to work to make this kind of money back home. I'm telling you, girls, at least three months for tonight's earnings,' one of the girls exclaims. We all nod with agreement, each one of us thinking about our own story.

'Of course, these kinds of nights happen pretty seldom, and usually our activities are more disgusting and energy-consuming,' Natalia jumps in. 'Nevertheless, since I started doing this, I've actually stopped feeling as cheap and insecure as I did while I was doing a "proper" job ...'

Masha interrupts Natalia by walking into the kitchen. She is unusually sober and in a horrible mood. She grabs a bottle of water from her shelf in the fridge and looks around.

'What are you looking at, bitches? It was the worst night ever! I couldn't even get drunk – had to hold the umbrella for those two brainsick fools all night long.'

We all look down, trying to suppress our drunken, hysterical laughter, until she throws her 'Whatever! I am going to sleep' into our midst and goes back to her room.

9

Unfortunately, this kind of night happens seldom in Luxembourg. Usually the job is a case of simple perversion and stress.

The owners pack the girls like sardines into their clubs, making the business unhealthily competitive. To keep the establishment optimally profitable, they 'motivate' the girls with an implicit rule, called a daily minimum norm: the €250 that each of us has to make for the bar per shift. There are no exceptions, even when there are no clients in the club. If we don't make money, they do not pay us a salary; if we do not improve our trade in the couple of days that follow, they fire us and send us back home. This shady but tangible undertaking never gets mentioned in the contract – the girls are faced with these 'terms and conditions' only when they get to Luxembourg.

Most of them are already jammed with debt on arrival: they pay the agent to organise access to the club (this usually costs between $500 and $1,000), and they pay for their flights, which include a trip to the Luxembourgish embassy in Moscow and the trip to Luxembourg itself – another $700 or $800. Obviously, they can't simply look around and say, 'Hmmm … I don't like it here. I am going back home,' then catch the next plane and face their creditors with fuck-all in their pockets. So, the 'unlucky shift', 'quiet business' or 'difficult client' options are, most of the time, simply not available. Instead, the dancers get so desperate to bag the damn champagne that if the customer asks them to do the Miller Plus[2], each one of them would do it without hesitation.

This setup results in another bummer: spoilt customers, or, frankly speaking, hard-to-please, twisted assholes.

You may think, what's the big deal? The girl is pretty, friendly, readily on tap. The customer is usually there for a reason too, which is not to check whether there are any new cocktails on the menu. Thus, the give and take between the parties should

---

2 Leap in acrobatics – double back somersault with double full twists.

be free of complications. A case of joy and pleasure –
he finds the best fit for himself and spends his time
and money with the doll according to his fancy or
capabilities.

*Sounds awesome, huh? But so fucking far away
from the real, perverse, stuffed-with-freaks-and-cheap-
desperate-whores-like-me place that is Luxembourg ...*

In reality, to get picked, the girl has to be very
creative. She has to be quick enough to get to the
customer before the others. The best way to do
that is always to face the entrance and never switch
your brain to standby mode – not that easy, when
the waiting time for a client can sometimes stretch
to hours. The more vigilant you are, the better your
chances of identifying and/or classifying the spender,
and acting accordingly.

The quickest way to approach the customer is
called, jokingly among the girls, roller skating –
you'd be surprised at the speed a girl can reach while
wearing extremely high heels and moving elegantly,
especially when she sees a high roller. Let's take me,
as an example: as soon as the client shows up at the
door, I get off my chair and glide towards him before
I even recognise him. Then, if – unfortunately – the
guy wants to take a leak, I walk behind him to the
bathroom, guard the door, and then accompany him
to where he chooses to sit, making sure that I am the
first to try my luck with him.

After the girl wins the opportunity to talk to a potential purchaser, she has only five minutes to excite his curiosity, to make him choose her and spend his money on champagne.

There are a few ways of doing it successfully.

She can be irresistibly beautiful, with big boobs, long legs, a firm ass, long and shiny hair, a sharp brain, a great personality, knowledge of the language the client prefers to speak, a huge fan of anal and an antagonist of condoms. In other words, she has to be perfect.

If this foolproof set of attributes doesn't apply, the entertainer can diagnose the client's preferences and secret desires before she approaches him, then provide whatever it is he needs – which means she has to be a psychic and a good actress. She must grasp what the man wants and transform, consistently, into a woman-vamp, innocent schoolgirl, or whatever it is that would match his fantasies. (Don't forget: she's got only five minutes)

If the second scenario is also not applicable, and the girl doesn't want to play Russian roulette with her small chance of guessing and fulfilling the customer's needs perfectly, she also can promise him something extra. Let's say hard-core anal, or that she will swallow his cum, or – even worse – that she will be a kamikaze and let him screw her without a rubber. Of course, many girls try to fool the client and not fulfill these promises of spicy undertakings, but most of the time the customer will complain to the manager, who always solves the dispute by deducting the amount from the girl's salary.

So, you have to be really smart, pushy and creative to be a successful hooker – oops, sorry: entertainer – in Luxembourg. Oh, and don't forget the Miller Plus …

10

Both of my sisters are doing pretty well, compared to the other girls. I am actually impressed with Lena's ability to bamboozle the clients and with Natalia's readiness to do almost anything when it comes to money. It's interesting; they both lack these qualities in real life and real relationships: Lena can never manipulate or control her men and always turns out to be the giver, whereas Natalia, after that blood-sucking affair with her boss, can never compromise or tolerate the shortcomings of her infrequent, and usually short-lived, relationships.

The night Lena first introduces me to her craftiness is one of those ill-fated shifts in which nearly all of the girls have a good run but Lena and me. We are sitting, downcast, at the bar when two guys walk in and head towards us. We smile, introduce ourselves and learn that they are Paulo and Fernando, from Portugal, and that they don't speak any English, or even French. The conversation is limited, but Lena doesn't shilly-shally. She explains – with just two words, one finger and the menu – that one hour of sex upstairs costs €250 each and includes a bottle of champagne.

The guys exchange a few remarks in their native language, then Paulo explains in gestures that they want *tak-tak* but they can't pay that much and would like to have two girls for the price of one bottle. *Tak-tak* appears to mean sexual intercourse, which we interpret from the recognisable movement of his hips that follows each use of this linguistic unit. Then, Fernando proudly points at the menu and adds that they can pay for two *demi-bouteilles* if that would suit us better.

Lena tries to suppress her irritation, smiles, and patiently explains to them again that *tak-tak* is possible only upstairs and that it is the club's policy to allow only one girl for one bottle. Then she points at the area where we entertain for the *demi-bouteilles*, lilts 'tak-tak ... la-bas ... pas possible[3]' and apologetically spreads her hands as if saying, 'Sorry guys, even if we

---

3 French, '*Tak-tak* ... there ... impossible'

wanted to help, there is nothing we can do, so if you want to fuck you will have to splash out'.

They exchange a few more words in Portuguese, then Paulo clarifies that they are okay with not going upstairs, but that they still want *tak-tak* and they will pay the price of the *demi-bouteille*, pointing again at the menu.

Lena wholeheartedly but almost voicelessly curses in Russian with a big smile on her face, saying something like, 'You are stupid and tight-assed idiots who get what they deserve,' then loudly announces, 'Okay!'

I almost fall off my chair and turn to my sister with big surprise in my eyes. She smiles at me and winks, indicating that I must not worry and just follow her lead.

Fernando grins in anticipation and juicily tongues his lips. At the same time, Paulo suspects there is something wrong and starts shaking his head, manifesting his doubt about her sudden go-ahead. Lena smirks confidently, steps closer to Paulo, pressing her breasts against his arm, and purrs into his ear, '*Tak-tak* ... *demi-bouteille* ... okay.' Then, after a tasty pause that is filled with Paulo's mistrust and suspicion, continues, '*Apres* ... *changer* ... *tak-tak*[4]' followed by gestures that without a doubt mean that my sister is insane. Besides, she promises them sex in

---

4   French, 'After ... change ... *tak-tak*'

the semi-private lounge, which we can't do; on top of that, she suggests that we swap partners at some stage!

You should see their faces! As soon as the images of Lena's tale swallow up their minds, all reason and common sense desert even Paulo.

They quickly swipe their cards and a few minutes later we are hugging on the two couches, not far from each other – me with Fernando and Lena with Paulo.

If the lounge area wasn't dimmed out to the extent that over the distance of a meter we couldn't really see each other, we would look like two couples who are madly in love, with chilled bottles of champagne in ice buckets, in full readiness for the half an hour of lust that Lena has promised the men.

Fernando starts kissing me, intensely pushing in his tongue and greedily smashing against my body as if there is no tomorrow. I let him do it, but respond by moving as frigidly as I can, trying to keep the moment at which he eventually decides to drop his pants as far away as possible. At the same time, my crazy sister moans excessively and passionately, 'Oh, *mon amour*[5],' making it extremely difficult to keep the fellow cool.

What is wrong with you, Lena?! Why can't you just shut up?! I am so angry that all I want right now is to get up and smack her in the head!

---

5 French, 'Oh, my love!'

After ten minutes of impulsive foreplay, and a few seconds before it's too late, Lena exclaims, '*Non! Tres chaud! Tres chaud! Changer!*'[6]

The guys priggishly smile at each other in a fever of excitement and let us swap places. And we start our foreplay all over again, but this time me with Paulo, and Lena with Fernando, wasting the precious half an hour. When the next ten minutes are finished, Lena pushes Fernando away, angrily looks at Paulo and me, and clamours, '*Jaloux! Tres jaloux. Mon amour! Changer! Changer!*'[7] We swap again and waste the last ten minutes the same way. Precisely half an hour later, my sister pushes her *amour* away and stiffly proposes that the men buy another bottle, because, 'Ooopsy!', their time is up.

Obviously, they can't afford another session. A wave of annoyance coats the dialogue in which they most probably share the realisation that they have just been fooled. To avoid complaints, Lena takes Paulo's phone number and promises to go on a date with him, which is as generous and fake as the offer she made them half an hour ago.

Our hot dates leave the club with a disappointment that they overlay with miserly smiles, thinking about the possibility of seeing my sister outside the club.

---

6   French, 'No! Very hot! Very hot! Change!'
7   French, 'Jealous! Very jealous. Love! Change! Change!'

Trust me, Lena gives me an even bigger shock than the one our not-so-bright-clients just received! I would never have imagined that she was capable of something like that …

A few days later, Natalia bowls me over with her working style as well, putting me in the same stupor as my middle sister had. I see her chatting to the guy at the bar, as if they've been friends for some time already, and finishing the second *piccolo*. Then she waves to me. I approach. She introduces us and asks if he wouldn't mind me joining them. His name is J.P., which is short for Jean-Paul or Jean-Pierre; I don't remember exactly. He happens to be a friendly and compliant guy, who, without hesitating, asks the barman to open a *piccolo* for me too.

As soon as we finish our first toast of the new acquaintance, and have a little chit-chat about the shared resemblances of and the differences between us three sisters, Natalia hugs J.P., putting her head on his shoulder while wrapping him in a playfully seductive look. She asks, 'Do you think you want to do it?'

J.P. blushes and awkwardly looks away, but Natalia tightens her hug and continues in the same manner, 'Hey, baby, you must stop with your endless modesty and use this opportunity, though that red colour looks very cute on your face. Let's do it! You will never have another two sisters who are as beautiful and as devoted, and who are ready to jump into your fantasy world and make it really ...' she pauses, widens her smile and then finishes, '... really special for you.' I have no clue what Natalia is talking about but I keep smiling and nodding my head, showing that I am one hundred per cent in. This time he looks at both of us and says, 'I want to do it, but let's have a few more drinks first.'

Natalia smiles, 'Sure.' I nod again. We order more champagne for ourselves and a double whisky for J.P.

The alcohol is doing its job. Less than an hour later, J.P. stops blushing and even starts telling us some dirty jokes. At the same time, he becomes so confident, or I would say so drunk, that he puts his hand under my skirt and softly but possessively smashes my ass underneath it, while whispering something flirtatious into Natalia's ear.

Another few double whiskies later, J.P. stands up and drunkenly babbles something indistinct but apparently very clear to my sister, because she jumps off her stool too and pulls him upstairs. While he is unsteadily swiping his credit card, I try to slip away to the bathroom, but get caught by Natalia, who whispers, 'Don't go anywhere, we'll need it in a few minutes'. And before I manage to put two and two together and realise what we're about to do, she drags us both into the room.

In Natalia's words, my role for the next hour is very simple. I am supposed to pee in J.P.'s mouth while he is getting a blowjob from my sister. She explains this in a way that sounds like she has just asked me to go to the shop and get a baguette for breakfast, nothing more!

We start with the ordinary threesome foreplay, kissing and undressing each other. I keep swilling down one glass after another in between the caressing and smooching, trying to accept the inevitable and help out my bladder. Some time later, Natalia slips down onto her knees and starts sucking him. I take my shoes off and climb on the couch, standing with my legs wide open so that J.P. is positioned right between them with my pussy on his face. He drops his head on the back of the couch and opens his mouth in readiness to consume. Everything is set for J.P.'s fantasy incarnation but my bladder.

... oh my fuck, I actually cannot do it!

Have you ever tried to pee into a man's mouth, standing naked on the couch while your sister is sucking his balls and watching you do it? My brain cannot agree with where I have chosen to empty my bladder, and refuses to send the signal to my urinary tract!

After a battle of some time, I eventually manage to relieve myself and water my new friend with my warm excretion. Our wishful thinker swallows it, instantly ejaculates and falls asleep.

'Here we are,' my sister comments without surprise, 'every time the same story!'

Natalia explains that we are not going to wake him up until the hour is over. We just sit there naked, next to our zonked-out sleeping beauty, drinking champagne and quietly talking about everyday stuff.

It probably looks insanely peaceful from the outside …

As soon as the hour is finished, Natalia wakes him up and starts to tear him into pieces. 'Baby, how could you do that to us! Two horny sisters, and you, selfish animal, just fell asleep on us! Now, you owe us both a great orgasm at the same time … Let's take another bottle and do it!'

To my big surprise, the man, half-drunk, half-asleep, nods guiltily and reaches for his wallet. Natalia goes to call the waiter to swipe the card, while I cover his naked body with his shirt. The manager shows up in a few seconds with the card machine and another two bottles. The payment goes through and we are left in the room alone again.

J.P. looks wide awake and ready for the action to resume. But after another glass of bubbly he passes out again during a super-passionate kiss with Natalia. We let him sleep. Another hour later, Natalia wakes him up. She is fibbing that he was incomparably good and that whatever he did to us was the best experience we'd ever had. He smiles and nods with absolutely misplaced complacency, then lets us make him drink some coffee and send him home with €1,500 less in his bank account.

Without a doubt, what I witness shakes me up, but also kind of makes me feel proud of my sisters. It is clear that they have been polishing this craft – trying to understand what the client wants, to discover his weaknesses and use them to get control over the situation, and to make him pay. Even though I have no idea how to do all that, I definitely know that I can master it with time – if I will use my pussy together with my brain ...

11

About a week after Lena's devoid-of-compassion tutorial and Natalia's fetishistic assignment, I also had a shift that would turn any of the girls green with envy – I made €400 in one night.

What's more, for the first time in my life I experienced an orgy. The wild gathering consisted of four participants: two clients, me and another of my colleagues, who, as it turned out later, used to be a man. Also, there was a lot of champagne, magic white powder, and at least two dozen condoms, which the *garçon* was shyly but desperately borrowing from the other girls around the club when ours ran out.

Nobody in the room knew that there was a trans-sexual among us until the last hour of the night ...

Her name was Claudia – by passport, Murat Kaya, Turkish citizen, 23 years old. A beautiful, intelligent and very feminine woman; no wonder none of us, for the whole night of our promiscuity, noticed anything abnormal. She, or at that stage he, was born in a small town somewhere in Eastern Anatolia, and by the age of twelve had already realised that nature had made a cruel mistake ... He was a woman in a man's body. Of course, Murat never shared his thoughts and feelings, not even with his family. He secretly gathered information and quickly learnt that there were many people like him all over the world. And even though his hometown was not the best place to live with such a 'malformation', at least the boy knew he was not alone. As soon as Murat turned eighteen, he received a passport. He headed to Istanbul, and then moved to Europe, where his problem had a solution – even though this involved a series of expensive tests and surgeries. After a few years of hard work and savings, he could eventually afford the transformation from an unhappy fellow full of complexes to an attractive and confident woman.

Everything was working out well for Claudia, except for the legalities. By Turkish law she couldn't change her gender and acquire a new identity. Moreover, as the holder of a passport in the name of Murat, she couldn't go back home and visit her family, because as soon as she reached the Turkish border she would be detained and forced to serve military duty – regardless of her long, blond hair and magnificent D cup under her sweater …

Anyway, as moving as this story is, it's not the one I want to tell you …

My off-the-wall night starts when the two fellows, my future orgy team, walk into the club at the beginning of the shift. They're already remarkably tipsy. I'm sitting at the bar right at the spot where they land for their first drink. I greet them with a wide smile, 'Hello guys! How are you?'

One of them turns and looks at me like I'm some importunate nuisance, pulls an arrogant face and turns back to his friend, talking and laughing. I angrily kill the remains of my cigarette in the ashtray, throw in a half-voiced 'Придурки!⁸' and leave the rude twosome. I've got a show to dance in less than twenty minutes, so I need to go upstairs to my room to get changed into my show-garb of a nurse with a heart-shaped stethoscope.

My music starts and I step onto the stage. The guy who just turned me down so meanly notices me, and interrupts the girl who is trying to hook up with him, in the same cocky way as he did with me just a few minutes ago. He gets up from the table where his friend is already talking to Claudia, and, spellbound, moves towards the stage saying something I can't hear. But I can read his lips: 'Wow! She is hot!'

---

8 Russian, 'Jerks!'

Through my whole performance, he stares at me as if I were Salma Hayek who had come down from Hollywood, and as if it was his lifelong dream to meet me, I mean her, from the moment he'd first watched the legendary *From Dusk till Dawn*.

What an idiot! A few minutes ago he didn't find me attractive and now look at him! He is drooling all over the place!

I haven't even changed back into my dress after the show when the *garçon* knocks on the door of my room and tells me that two customers are settled in *séparé* number three – the biggest private room in the club – waiting for me.

I hurriedly fix my make-up, spray some perfume and rush down the stairs.

There are two big couches in the room that face each other. They are separated by a considerably big wooden coffee table, which is already decorated with two shiny buckets full of ice, a golden bottle's neck sticking out of each of them. One couch is occupied by my new admirer, who is looking at me with pure adoration in his eyes. On the other one is Claudia with the second guy. Those two are so busy kissing and caressing each other that they haven't even noticed me walking in.

'My name is Chris,' my new bad-mannered friend tells me while filling my glass to the top, 'and I must tell you it's a beautiful show you did down there …' I thank him and nervously swallow the bubbly.

The idea of us sharing the room is making me uncomfortable. I am desperately looking for the right words in my head to convince him to relocate to another *séparé*.

'Chris, would you like …?' Before I can finish, he leans towards me, pushing me to lie down.

'Oh yes, Julia, I would like …' and he starts covering my body with clumsy kisses while pulling my little strapless red dress down to the floor. And as I turn away to let him wet my neck rather than my mouth, I see naked Claudia rhythmically moving on the top of the also already undressed friend of Chris.

Okay. I get it … we are not going to move to another room …

For some time, we just intensively hump in front of each other; it feels absolutely insane to be watched while having sex and eyeing the other couple doing the same in front of you.

By the time we're onto bottle number three, a few hours later, all four of us have ended up on one couch, creating an agglomeration of human bodies that is moving wildly and making sluttish noises.

I start getting used to the weirdness until the *garçon*, who enters the room in the middle of our action to bring more champagne, ice or condoms, takes me right back to the point at which I'm shocked by witnessing and experiencing all of this …

Another few hours, and absolutely nothing feels strange to me anymore. We're so stoned that I hardly know where I am and what I am doing …

We drink, sniff and fuck, regularly changing positions and locations.

For the last few hours of our explicit freestyle race, we are incapable of doing anything more than just lying naked on the couches, staring at the ceiling, smoking, talking crap and laughing like we are 13 years old again, spending the night in summer camp. It is now that Claudia shares her story with us. The guys are so drunk that they are moved almost to tears, ignoring the fact that they just did all sorts of things that straight men would never voluntarily go through.

That night, we opened more than 16 bottles of champagne, and drank most of them. I didn't even remember how I got to my bed.

12

Ow … that hurts!

I try to open my eyes and understand what woke me up. Natalia is in my room, walking around, picking my clothes up off the floor while talking to me. Despite the time – already about 5 p.m. – her every word feels like a hammer against my head. I quickly shut my eyes again.

What the hell is she doing here?

Apparently, the fact that I am incapable of doing any kind of activity, including having a conversation, is obvious only to me.

When I finally turn my brains on and understand what she is talking about, I can't believe my ears. She has actually come to lecture me about my alcohol and drug use and how much damage it can cause to my life and health!

Seriously?

She refuses to notice when I turn away, covering my head with the blanket in irritation. She just goes on and on about the risks to my future wellness. Then, she ignores my 'Please Nata, not now, my head will explode!' and jumps in, dressing me down in her favorite soapbox manner about how I should avoid drinking to excess and enumerating the ways in which we can fool the customers.

'Where is your wooden stick?'

Her tone is driving me mad. She is standing in front of me with my work purse open.

'Jul? Answer me. Where is it?'

I moan.

'I can see lipstick, condoms and chewing gum. Where is the fucking wooden stick I gave you?'

I can't believe it; she's actually raising her voice at me.

'I am not using the stupid stick. Leave me alone.'

My voice is hoarse from smoking too much last night.

'Why not?' she exclaims with fury. 'You know it helps to stay sober!'

I remember the day we arrived. She'd given me this wooden stick with a star-like tip, calling it a 'magic wand'. It came with a half-hour lecture on why we need to use it.

Apparently, if you stir the champagne in your glass with this stick, it goes flat faster. 'It's not a secret that the fizz speeds up the absorption of the alcohol into your bloodstream. This is a killer for us, Jul. So, all you have to do is stir it a few times,' she'd said, trying to appeal to my common sense.

'What is the point, sister? The fun is in getting drunk. Why delay it?' I'd jokingly answered, knowing that as soon as she left the room I would throw this piece of magic into the garbage. *Seriously, how else am I supposed to deal with doing this crazy job every day? I'm not Miss Perfect like you, Nata ...*

'Jul!'

She was losing it. And just like today, I decided not to make any further comments, to get her to leave faster.

'Very often, Jul, the amounts of alcohol you will have to consume are crazy. And you don't want to get sick on the client or pass out when you could make more money. Listen to me. You must try to drink as little as possible.'

I'd nodded, hoping that she was finally done with her useful tips and tricks. But she'd just carried on.

'Besides using the stick, you could also pour the swill onto the carpet, couch or curtains. On anything that can absorb liquid. Although,' she smiled, 'the client could easily detect this fraud. So the best way is to pour it right into the ice bucket when he leaves to use the bathroom ...'

Natalia drags me back from my memories, handing
me a glass of water and two aspirins.

'My point is that if you continue drinking like
that, Jul, in a few months all the money you've earned
will have to be spent on gastroenterologists.'

Arghh … where do you even get these words from???
Why can't you just shut up and leave me alone?

'You think that drunkenness helps you to be
relaxed, funny and confident, but in fact it just makes
you lose control. How can you not understand that?'

I wrinkle my nose, trying to keep my head still –
the pain of every movement tortures me. But, again,
Natalia chooses not to notice my hangover suffering,
and continues, 'You were just lucky last night. Those
guys would have spent all of that money anyway,
even if you were a monkey. But if it had come to a
situation where you had to manipulate or influence
them to make them pay, you wouldn't have been
aware of it. You are always wasted, Jul.'

I am watching two tablets dissolve. I can't believe
that she is actually saying all this instead of just being
happy for my success last night!

'You're just jealous, Nata, aren't you?' I wheeze.

'Oh, please, Julia. Jealous of what? You literally
killing yourself? How long will you be able to carry
on like this?'

'Well, you don't really expect me to do this job
forever, right?' The bubbles of the fizzing aspirin are
tickling my nose while I down it in one gulp. 'And

what do you mean by losing control? Control over being fucked in front of other people, Miss I-do-everything-the-right-way? Guess what, Natalia – not everybody is perfect like you. Just deal with it! Jesus, my head is really going to explode now … Can't we leave this preaching for some other time? I am in pain and I need to start getting ready for work.'

'Whatever, Jul … I was just trying to be helpful', says Natalia, heading towards the door. Just before she leaves the room, she turns to me and adds, with a sarcastic smile, 'By the way, congratulations. You did extremely well last night.'

13

My loving sister Natalia induces the boss to change my shift to the daytime for the next month. She wants to save me from drugs and separate me from Masha.

Isn't it charmingly naïve?

The day run finishes at 10 p.m. As soon as it's over, I go to the nightclubs with different clients, who are more than happy to supply me with a hit in the hopes of free intercourse after the party.

Nice try, Nata. But I'll find a way if I want to …

Unfortunately, working in the day also means working with the freakiest freaks in Luxembourg. In this particular club, what also helps to bring these pathetic bastards in is a big screen that runs non-stop hardcore porn without sound.

It is the end of my first week on the day shift, which hasn't gone too well for me business-wise. I wasn't quick enough (the other girls were really good at roller skating), or the clients simply didn't want me. Yesterday, already, I could see the manager giving me sidelong glances, so I am really under pressure to make it work today. While I am busy thinking about my difficulties, the door slowly opens and the first customer walks in.

He is a pale, tall fatso in his late 80s – yes, still a frequent visitor to such places, and yes, who still regularly goes upstairs for nookie! Okay, maybe the word 'goes' is too strong; he battles to move, with the help of his walking stick or sometimes even a barman. Among the girls, his nickname is Death.

When he shuffles in and heads to the bar, all the girls sigh together with dislike and turn away from him. Despite the tough competition, not one of them tries to get to Death first. To me, the dodderer looks like a harmless dude. My first guess why the girls have given him such a discouraging name is that he looks like he is going to die very, very soon. Nice try, but far from the real reason …

Apparently, he always likes to try the new girls, so it is my turn to get to know him better.

The barman, Franc, is chatting to Death. He waves to me, and without extra words, directs us to the stairs. When we finally reach the next floor, grandpa and I make ourselves comfortable on the two-seater couch in a small, square room with a coffee table, dustbin and miniature hand-wash basin hanging on the wall, which is papered with dull flowers. Franc opens and pours the champagne, using the best manners and etiquette, while engaging in a little talk with my playmate, politely pretending that he is interested in a conversation. At the same time, I am trying to calm myself with the idea that if Death can hardly move his limbs (you should see him climbing up the stairs, with barmen behind him as a backup in case he collapses), any further activity should not go beyond an innocent chat or, at most, some modest cuddling.

As soon as the door closes behind the barman, Death starts peeling his clothes off. I freeze in stupor.

The words 'Take off your dress' bring me back to my disturbing reality. With credulous optimism, I down a glass of champagne and obey.

What follows is worse than a nightmare …

For the whole hour that we spend together, he deep-kisses me on my mouth, forcing his sour, mucus-covered tongue down my throat and sadistically biting my lips. I cannot even describe the smell that his whole body emits, but I finally figure why the girls gave him his nickname. He stinks, as if he is already dead and rotting from the inside. All I can think about is how to suppress the urge to vomit.

He likes it harsh – asks me to squeeze his nipples hard and pinches mine exhaustively too. A stifled 'ouch' uncontrollably slips out while my face distorts from the pain. The son of a bitch sulkily pushes me away and wheezes with irritation: 'Don't you like it?' Clearly, to earn the bottle, I don't only have to participate in this aversion – the pretense that I'm having the best time of my life is also required. I force a smile and assure him that I am certainly turned on, but it is just a little bit too intense for me. He 'hmmms' and goes back to his sadistic manipulations.

He keeps pressing my face into his full, hanging breasts, forcing me to bite and suck his nipples, while poking his crooked fingers into my dry pussy, scratching it with his nails. I try to keep my eyes closed: his pale and wizened skin is covered with blue knots of varicose veins, which doesn't make it any easier for me to fight the reflex to puke.

This revolting scene ends up with me on my knees, sucking the disgustingly soft, eighty-year-old cock, until Death finally comes in my mouth. I wash down the thick and smelly fluid with another glass of champagne and genuinely smile. Incredible … I feel happy.

The torture is over, but not my amazement. The dodderer is so tired after the session that I actually have to dress him. Think of a hundred kilograms of calf's-foot jelly that has to be pushed into a human's clothes. It takes me some time. After I've worked up a good sweat, the barman helps Death to get down the stairs. And he leaves the club alive. Again.

I go to the toilet and wash my hands and face. I rinse my mouth and chew bubblegum, but cannot get rid of the rotten smell and taste in my mouth.

I cannot stop thinking about why I didn't simply tell Death to fuck off. It's not as if I have five little kids waiting for me at home and no money to buy them food. What can I say? I guess it's life … You never know what a lack of money, poor social security, alluring TV shows with their fabulous people and luxury things, a desperate desire to have a decent life, and young age can do to you.

Still deep in thought, I go down to the bar and ask for a shot of tequila. Even though we are not allowed to drink any alcoholic beverages except champagne with the clients, Franc nods and pours me a double.

14

It is the third month of our trip. Lena calls me to meet for coffee.

This month she had to move to another club. Our boss wanted to hire a few new girls, and Lena simply wasn't his favourite. Her new club, 'Angels' House', is somewhere in the suburbs, close to the German border, about 30 minutes away by bus.

The place is dodgy and we mock it by calling it 'House of Slumbers'.

It is a small, country-style bar with a female owner. To save money, she is the barman as well as the only waitress, which makes the place a total fuck-up considering that she's a 'striking' boozer too. Usually she doesn't hire more than five or six girls. Four of them work constantly, and also drink like fish; the remaining one or two are new girls every month, like Lena, to refresh the trashiness.

What tops off the place is the shiny lever on the bar. Girls are allowed to enjoy (or, rather, abuse) the limitless beer on tap. Obviously, the alky-owner looks better from an outsider's point of view when everyone around her is drunk too. By the time the first clients start entering the club, the bar looks like the Land of Nod.

This is the first time I am going to see Lena in three weeks. Besides the fact that lately I spend all my spare time on catching some Z's after my nightly festivities, Lena seldom has a chance to get to town.

The snag is the club owner. She lives in one of the rooms on the second floor of 'Angels' House', together with the working girls. The wooden floor in the hallway is old and creaky. So, while she sleeps to recover from her crapulence, the crazy woman doesn't allow her employees to come out of their rooms until noon.

The public buses only pass by every hour. The first bus after noon comes at 1 p.m. Lena's shift starts at 5 p.m. The four hours of available time is too little to go to town, considering that one of them is wasted in transit. The girls also have to get ready for their shift, but there is only one shower for all six of them, making it impossible to keep their preparation time short.

Imprisonment in their rooms applies not only to the girls' going out of the building; while the boss is sleeping, they can't even use the bathroom or the kitchen. The latter is in a very small room without a fridge, a table, or even a sink. Girls have to wash the dishes in the bathtub. The only equipment that makes the room look like a kitchen is an old electric kettle and oven, which hardly heats up. The rest of the space is stuffed with old, dirty tableware and food products that are stored everywhere: a few overloaded shelves and even the floors.

Lena is very lonely there, which is why she called me and kept insisting on a reunion, saying that she misses me a lot and has something to tell me. I couldn't say no. She sounded almost desperate on the phone.

When I get to the place, our fave café on the Place de Paris, Lena is already waiting for me. She rises from the cane-chair, hugs and kisses me. On my how-are-you-sis she tiredly sighs, 'Don't even ask ...' then drops back onto her chair and sighs again.

'I haven't slept all night. We had a situation ...' She pauses to role her eyes.

I wave to the waiter to bring me the same, while pointing at Lena's already cold cappuccino and keeping an oh-my-god-what-happened expression on my face.

Turns out that her roommate Sasha was having some kind of a heart attack last night, and when one of the girls tried to call an ambulance, their alky-boss prohibited her because 'it would cost too much'.

Really, what a bitch!

'She scared me so much, but luckily it didn't end badly, I managed to find corvalol drops in one of the girls' medical aid kits, and after some time Sasha's chest pain calmed down and she fell asleep.'

'Thank God she is fine.' I fake my concern, thinking of my bed and how nice it would be to jump back in it for a few more hours.

'Yes! *She* was fine,' Lena continues with more indignation, 'but not me! You know, seeing a fainting person is enough to make me faint myself ...'

Oh yes, I do know ...

It is not news that Lena is very wary and panicky. On top of that, sometimes she has cases of fainting for real. She would wake up in the middle of the night in a cold sweat, feeling nauseous. She would get out of bed to go to the bathroom, and on the way there, she would zonk out and fall onto the floor. A few times, she smashed her face badly. That's why she had to learn to control herself and not to jump out of bed whenever she woke up feeling groggy. Instead, she would just slide off the bed and crawl into the bathroom, so that if she did faint, she would already be near the floor, avoiding a dangerous fall.

There is no particular reason for these incidents; at least the doctors couldn't find one. But most of the time it happens when she drinks or eats to excess – even just a little, which most of us would still consider to be moderation.

'I couldn't make myself sleep at all last night ...' her voice right now is full of so much irritating drama that I want to just flick her forehead.

'But don't worry, Jul. It's all okay now.'

'Good, Len. I am glad you both are well now ...'

I was not worried at all, although I felt sorry for Lena. Of the three of us, the drinking-a-lot situation was the most difficult for her. But I know she was somehow managing, keeping her 'moderation' in the safe levels. After a few incidents in Luxembourg, during her first contract already, Lena also learnt how to drink without drinking. Every time she had more than two glasses of champagne, she'd go to the toilet, carefully put two fingers down her throat and eject the contents of her stomach. The only things she had to remember were to keep it quiet, not to forget the make-up bag to touch up after the procedure, and, of course, a mint or chewing gum.

Phew ... yuck!

This may seem like a good solution for our problem of having to drink a lot every day, but only at first glance. Believe me: imagine forcing yourself to throw up several times a night, which wouldn't be a big deal if you were bulimic and vomiting food, but I am talking about puking pure acid out of your stomach, mixed with sour champagne. Aside from the cocktail being extremely nasty, it also burns your throat and gullet.

The girls like me, who can tolerate big amounts of alcohol and other stuff, try never to use this option.

As I try hard not to fall asleep sitting right there in the café, I notice that my sister is, regardless her weariness, unusually twitchy, and that her eyes sparkle oddly.

Something is going on with her … and I don't like it …

After the waiter brings us another two cappuccinos, this time decaf, Lena cradles her cup with both hands and smiles at me.

'Jul, there is something else I wanted to talk to you about.'

No fucking way you are pregnant again! I think, but say only, 'What is it?'

'There is this customer I met a few weeks ago,' Lena goes on. 'Michel. He is from Paris, handsome, fit, 43 years old and not married.' She pauses, looks inside her cup and adds, 'At least, that is what he told me. But I believe him, Jul. Why would he lie?'

He would lie for the same reason as all your previous boyfriends did. Because this is what you want to hear, my hopelessly child-like sister.

'On the first night,' she continues, 'he bought six bottles of Dom Perignon and didn't even touch me. We spent all night talking about love and life. He kept looking into my eyes, saying that I was the most beautiful creature he had ever seen.'

'Wow! Six bottles?' I whisper, counting in my head how much my sister made that night.

'You would not believe it, but a week later Michel came back! He asked if I would like to join him for dinner. Of course I said yes. He paid the club the fine for my absence, and took me to a fine restaurant. Then he suggested that we go to his suite in the five star hotel, to continue the night ...' She looks down and bites her lip. 'You know, strawberries and champagne in a beautiful hotel room with a gorgeous view and a handsome man who adores you ... it was an amazing night ... like a dream, Jul. A fairy tale!'

I sigh with admiration. 'You are definitely one lucky bitch, Len!'

She sighs too. 'But there is something else ...' Her voice drops and she falls silent in hesitation. I can see she is struggling to find the courage to say what she wants to say.

Oh no! You are definitely knocked up! goes through my head and I lean over the table and ask, trying to hide the irritation, 'What, Len?'

'The only little thing –' she stops and looks down again '– is ... hmmm ... he wore red fishnet stockings

under his €3,000 suit; he didn't take them off until
we'd finished making love.'

'No way! Len, are you serious?' I start laughing and
my sister goes as red as the bright cashmere sweater
she is wearing.

'Stop laughing!' she exclaims. 'I think I love him.'
When I notice the tears in her eyes I cover my face
with my hands and try to cease my laughter. I know
what 'I love him' means in Lena's interpretation – 'I
am ready to marry him and have kids ...' And that
if she is not knocked up yet, she is going to be soon.

'Come on Len, what do you want me to say? He
is a perfect customer! I know you've already dreamt
about you two getting married, but don't freak out
straight away. Sometimes absolutely abnormal things
can, with time, become surprisingly normal. So what?
Stockings? He seems like a nice guy to me anyway.
What you should do is wear stockings yourself next
time too.' And we burst into laughter, together this
time.

I walk her to the bus station and we talk more
about her new admirer. Then Lena suddenly shoots,
'Natalia told me you were fighting a lot lately.'

'Never mind,' I brush her off. 'You know Natalia.'

But Lena isn't going to let go. 'You know, Jul, you
must talk to somebody, get help, besides you know
we are always there for you.' She says this as if she is
my therapist and I am some kind of mental patient.

Now I don't even try to suppress my irritation. 'I am fine, Lena, just smoking dope sometimes. Not a big deal! It's not like I am some kind of junkie! Relax! Stop listening to Natalia! And just make sure you use condoms, so you don't repeat your previous mistakes.'

15

It is a few months since we left Ukraine, but it only took me a few hours – not even days – to adapt to the grown-up world. I feel so cool and easy. I enjoy my financial freedom; I guess that is the first thing that changes any child into an adult. I love the fact that I am in charge. The unknown future and its responsibilities infect me with a bit of fear and rash excitement.

The only paradox that can't stop stirring in my head is why on earth am I so morally comfortable with what I am doing? I do not feel ashamed or dirty because I am a pro.

Don't get me wrong: I am not trying to promote this job, even though it can be the best recipe for many women for how to find the damn G-spot. We all know that practice makes perfect. I am not going to be insincere either and tell you that I fuck for money because I love sex. I do love sex, but the clientele does not come from my imaginary perfect world. The guys who are more often part of my reality are ugly, fat, smelly or sweaty. Hookers usually aren't in a position to be picky, because they have already made their choice – the money. What's more, this trade wouldn't be my first choice if there were other well-paid jobs available. Trust me, if teachers earned the same as sex traders, I would not hesitate to change my clientele from adults to the under-aged.

So, this is not an attempt to find the merits or reveal the evils of this profession, or to justify my choice. It is about my curiosity. I am curious about my ease with what I do.

I don't think it is my sisters' fault, although they did set an example. I was okay with this even before I learned what kind of job they did in Luxembourg. The first time I had sex in exchange for the agreed-on-in-advance amount was when I was sixteen.

During the summer holidays, my school friend Sveta and I took jobs as waitresses in one of the resorts on the Black Sea. It was a great opportunity to get tanned, hang out and make a little bit of money. We made friends with all of the staff, including three security guards – who, although a lot of fun, annoyingly hassled us.

Once, the barman, Sergey, called both of us for a little chat. 'Dolls, would you like to make some extra cash? There are two men from Moscow. They want some fun, but because their wives and kids are here too, the fun must be quiet and decent. They saw you two on the beach and liked you. Tomorrow they are going fishing on the lake and would like you two to join them for few hours – one hundred dollars each,' he finished, and smiled.

I looked at Sveta. She was stunned. After a pause she threw 'No way!' at Sergey with disgust, and left the bar. Sergey confidently followed her leaving with his eyes, and a sarcastic 'Sure, princess. Go! Eventually you will get fucked by one of those callow guards anyway …' He turned to me with a questioning look and added, '… for free, of course.'

It was a surprise to me, but I didn't rise in revolt from the proposition. What was even more shattering – I totally agreed with the barman.

'How safe is it?'

'They are normal dudes; if they weren't, I wouldn't handle the negotiation.'

The next day, at about ten in the morning, one of them picked me up in his latest-model black Mercedes, a few kilometers away from our resort as we had agreed. I had never been taken for a drive in a car that stylish. It took us fifteen minutes to get to the peaceful glade with its small lake, where his friend, it turned out, was already fishing – for real.

'I will give you another hundred if you do my friend as well,' my driver announced with ease, as if we were talking about the weather. 'Your choice; we will not force you to do anything.'

It took me some time to convert two hundred bucks into *hryvni*. The sound of the anxious pulse in my head slowed my brain down. Nevertheless, the amount was equivalent to four months of my salary as a waitress, with tips. I tried to calm myself down; I made sure that my voice stayed firm and replied, 'Okay, but one at a time.' He nodded 'No problem,' then asked me to undress and to move to the back seat.

Before we started, my employer quickly took off his shorts and T-shirt, rolled a condom over his cock, and, before climbing into the car, wisely covered the leather seat with a beach towel.

We started with me on top of him. Very soon he got tired of my flat chest and lifted me up, turning me around at the same time. He pushed my head down, squashing my face into the leather that was now stripped of the towel, and bonked me from behind. He was rough but didn't hurt me; more importantly, it didn't take him long to come.

As soon as he was done, he mumbled 'Good girl, stay where you are,' put his shorts back on, and walked away towards the lake.

When his friend came to the car a few minutes later, I was lying on my back, bashfully covered with the towel. The friend was cool as a cucumber: he smiled, unzipped his shorts, wrapped his swollen member in rubber and climbed on top of me. It was my lucky day: he was even faster than his friend. Ten minutes of rhythmical rocking in the missionary position and I was free to go with two hundred bucks in my pocket.

The barman was right: the 'dudes' were 'normal', and one of the security guards did screw Sveta after all … for free.

When the summer ended and we went back home, Sveta started to complain about pain in her throat and discomfort when she urinated. The blood test showed the clap and a few other X-rated infections. When I asked her if they had used any protection, Sveta wiped her tears and blubbered in embarrassment that he had told her that he'd put on the condom, but it was dark and she couldn't see. She was too shy to check with her hand.

That summer story didn't shape my views about life: the barman's words were not news to me. So, I look for answers in the earlier stages of my life, but can't find any clues in my childhood either. We grew up in a friendly, strong and intelligent family; our parents had a healthy relationship. We were raised on Tolstoy and Dostoyevsky and steeped in the concepts of integrity and fairness. I think that my I-am-okay-with-being-a-pro attitude is simply a consequence of my observations of everyday life.

For example, my schoolmate Marina liked Anton from our group, but dated 24-year-old Misha who had his own business and decent wheels, and who picked her up after classes once in a while. That made Marina feel cooler than the rest of the girls in our class (including me), and successfully substituted Anton's great sense of humor.

Another great example was our neighbour, Dasha, from the fifth floor. She was my mother's kitchen-small-talk friend, and came for coffee and a few cigarettes almost every day. Most of their conversations ended up being about Dmitri, Dasha's husband, who, according to her, was a rare type of dickhead. He'd been involved with another woman for almost two years. On each visit, Dasha complained that she was tired of the life that was built on the lie, that she didn't even love 'the bastard' any more, and that she would have left him long ago if she had anywhere to go other than her mother's small apartment. Her mother lived somewhere on the outskirts of Kherson and drove her mad. These were good excuses for Dasha to continue living a life of no self-respect and constant complaints.

I saw many of these examples around me every day: because of social, economic and other circumstances, including low self-esteem, a fear of change, the belief that they didn't deserve better, or simply to gain any sort of advantage, women often entered into – or stayed in – relationships for reasons other than love or sexual attraction. My curious logic may not have been developed at the time, but I could not see the difference between this type of relationship and one in which women honestly named their monetary price.

I saw so many of these 'love affairs without love' that I became used to the concept and formed my okay-with-being-a-pro attitude. As I see it, the only difference between any hooker and our neighbour Dasha is that the former's 'labour hour' is the latter's lifetime.

16

I go to work in an annoyingly nasty mood. No wonder I am pissed off – besides the hangover from the previous night's booze-diving routine that doesn't want to simmer down, and although it's 5 p.m. and it still feels like my body has been thrown from the fifth floor onto the driveway, five minutes ago I received a text from one of my regulars.

Oh yes, he is one of the first clients whom I can proudly call 'my customer'.

The chap is in his fifties, in good shape, not bad looking but a repulsively unpleasant and sleazy man. He lives in Paris and, of course, is married. Two or three times a month he comes to Luxembourg for business and pleasure. When we first met in the club, about three months ago, he acted like a real gentleman: asked some neutral questions about my family and my life, trying really hard to show that he was interested in me, and not sex. He kept throwing lines like, 'Oh, all three of you are beautiful sisters! Your mother must be a gorgeous woman!' or 'You are an intelligent woman, Julia, you shouldn't be working here ...'

Blah-blah-blah ...

After twenty minutes of our causerie and a few glasses of champagne, he asked if I would like to join him upstairs, bought a bottle of Laurent-Perrier for €375, refusing to drink the shoddy swill the club sold for €250, and politely fucked me from behind. Before he left, he gave me his phone number and suggested that we meet outside of the club when next he was in town, offering a meal in a fancy restaurant, a room in a decent hotel and €300 for the night.

This overture sounded like a top-notch bargain to me, until our first 'date' ...

My Frenchman is one of those characters who never lets me out of his sight. He never stops hugging or touching me, or, more importantly, kissing me, usually with his wet tongue deep inside my throat. No matter what! While walking in the street, driving, sleeping, showering or even eating.

He loves to walk hand in hand through the Luxembourg streets and pull me every few minutes, clinching and grabbing me under the skirt or sweater, while constantly licking my mouth inside and out. Every red light we hit while driving to the hotel or restaurant he burrows through my tights and panties and plugs his fingers into my slit while searching with his tongue for my trachea. The bastard loves to join me in the shower, ignoring my protests and also insisting on us lathering and washing each other while, of course, kissing all the time … he never stops hugging me at night, groping my tits and my pussy even while I sleep.

Oh, and the most annoying part is the restaurants. He always sits next to me, periodically squeezing my thighs and deep-throat smooching while still chewing on his food. *Thinking about it makes me want to throw up instantly …* He keeps on gazing into my eyes and saying '*Je t'aime*'[9] while I fight the natural impulse to show the disgust on my face, smile instead and answer 'I love you too'.

Yuck …

Guess what the most revolting part of our 'dating' is? Of course it's sex. We fuck once or twice before going to sleep and usually twice in the morning – before and after breakfast. He cannot come without me stimulating his anus. Usually that involves my finger in his ass while he is fucking me on top, or

---

9   French 'I love you'

sometimes he just climbs above my face and makes me lick his asshole while he jerks himself off. *Yuck! Yuck! Yuck!*

After each of his visits I feel so squelchy and drained that the only thing that can pull me out of that depressed mental condition is intensive three-hour shopping therapy. A few hundred euro spent on shoes and clothes – that is the best medicine I've come up with so far.

Back to the SMS I received from the French sleazeball … He is arriving tonight and is going to stay for two days instead of his usual one-night visit. It's a Saturday night, so he will spend it in our cabaret with me. As soon as my shift is over, he will take me to some *magnifique*[10] French hotel, outside of Luxembourg City, somewhere on the border with Germany, where we can 'enjoy' each other in full, until Monday …

Fuck! That is at least 42 hours of excruciation for my mind and body!

He arrives at the club and we move to the semi-private lounge. The only thing I can think about, while nodding and smiling to some boring stories he is telling with the excitement of an eight-year-old, is the 42 hours I am going to have to get through. I guzzle the champagne, hoping it will help me.

---

10 French, 'magnificent'

Already pretty loaded with alcohol, I go to the bathroom where I bump into Masha. She looks at me and roars, 'What's wrong, my baby? You look like a piece of trash! Do you need some extra stimulus? It looks like the alcohol does not love you tonight.'

'Masha, nothing will work for me,' I weep drunkenly. 'I can't stand the sleaze-ball anymore! I don't need a stimulant; I need something that will switch off my brain for the next two days!'

'Let me think …' moans Masha. 'I have something that just might work for you.' She leaves the restroom.

A few minutes later, she returns with a small plastic bag with some blue pills in it, quickly hands it to me so my 'beloved' doesn't notice, whispers in my ear, 'Don't take more than two at a time,' and disappears.

I have no idea what is in the bag but swallow a few tablets without batting an eye. And then it comes … the world around me begins to modify. My arms, legs and eyelids get heavier … my attitude shifts too – from distressed and jerky to I-don't-give-a-fuck-what's-happening-to-me-at-all …

Feels good … I love it! I decide to make sure that this wonderful state will not leave me for as long as possible and have another two. I feel cool as a cucumber for a little longer, and then blank out.

I wake up the next day in my bed. I can't remember anything: how I got here or what happened the previous night. There is Lena, sitting next to my bed with a worried face, and Masha, in a hyper state, doing some cleaning in the room and irritably answering Lena's 'should we take her to the hospital?' questions: 'She is going to be fine, Lena. You should rather go to the mall and do some shopping and let your sister sleep. Stop worrying.' Judging by Masha's tone, she isn't saying this for the first time.

Apparently what happened was that some time after I had taken the third and fourth hit of Valium, I'd grasped my Frenchman's face with two hands, digging into his skin with my nails, and with an unblinking loony stare hissed something not very nice through my clenched teeth. Then, abruptly, dropped back on the couch. My eyes rolled back and white, frothy saliva started to come out of my mouth. Sleaze-ball got a fright and, while staring at me, kept shouting something like, 'Are you okay, my angel?'

What an idiot! Obviously I wasn't!

Masha immediately understood what had happen-ed, and with an 'I told you, not more than two at a time!' pulled me into the bathroom, where she pushed two fingers down my throat and made me puke, removing the excess of the sedatives.

When I'm finally able to switch on my brain and recalculate the outcome of the night, I genuinely smile.

I didn't make any cash over the weekend. The following day our boss barked at me, threatening to fire me if he found out about one more drug incident involving me. But I missed it! I missed the weekend from hell. I learnt that Valium and alcohol are not a good combination for my body. And that my sleaze-ball is probably angry, because I haven't received an SMS from him.

I wonder what I hissed at him ... something tells me it was not sweet and pleasant, taking into account that it was not me speaking but my psyche that was freed from abuse and suppression.

My joy doesn't last long, though. A week later my phone comes alive with a text from him. It informs me that he is sure that I was just not feeling well and didn't mean what I said. And that he'd be coming back the following week and would love to see me. Oh, and that he was having some difficulties with money and would not be able to pay me, but believed it wouldn't be a problem for us, because our relationship was built on genuine feelings ...

Yeah, right!

I get ecstatic. My greed, my desire to make more money, always pushed me to handle one more bout of torture and prevented me from stopping abusing myself and ceasing our meetings. But thanks to his greed, I no longer have a choice. I write back that there is absolutely fucking nothing on this earth that could make me spend even an hour with him for free, and that when he talks about our 'strong bond' it makes me sick.

He doesn't respond. I spend another couple of days feeling sunny and energetic. I even forget about him. However, on the night he was scheduled to arrive in Luxembourg, his visit to the club takes me by surprise.

Demonstratively, he takes another girl upstairs. On his way past, he throws something like, 'Venal two-faced bitch!' at me.

I look at him and smile. 'I know'.

I think to myself that even if he pours a barrel of crap over my head right now, I would still keep smiling, because there is only one cheerful thought that keeps swinging through my head – 'I am not the one who has to go upstairs with him!'

Alleluia!

17

It is just another weekend when my sisters and I meet for our Sunday lunch, which we try to do regularly to catch up on the latest news, especially now that Lena is working out of town. Considering our habit of sleeping late, we never gather earlier than three or four in the afternoon, and we usually drag lunch out into the evening. As I've never had sushi before we decide to go to a nice little Japanese place not far away from where Natalia and I are staying. No cabarets are open on Sundays, so it is the only day during the week on which we can get together and totally relax without watching the time and worrying about when our shift is going to start.

'I love this feeling,' I say while Lena shows me how to hold the chopsticks, 'of not having to rush to work after lunch ... I wish I was the daughter of a millionaire.' I sigh, losing myself in my delusional thoughts. 'I wouldn't need to work then ...'

'I'd rather be the wife of a millionaire', says Lena, also with a dreamy look on her face.

'Let's say you'd rather be a wife, no matter whose,' adds Natalia, and we giggle.

'By the way, Nata, I hear from Jul that you are dating somebody now!' Lena sounds very excited. She leans over the table and lowers her voice, 'A black guy?' A light blush covers her face.

'I'm not dating him, I'm just fucking him,' replies Natalia, and swallows a succulent salmon roll.

She explains that they met in the club. His name is Carlos and he is from Portugal. He plays semi-professional soccer, doesn't speak a word of English, and his French is even worse than Natalia's. He is good-looking, with a hot body, and is very young.

'He is only 19!' says my eldest sister. 'It feels like I am taking advantage of the kid!'

He bought her a *demi-bouteille* and acted like a gentleman, without asking her for anything in return but half an hour's company and a chat. Afterwards, he offered her €200 to join him at his place after work. Natalia agreed, telling us that he is so sexually attractive that she 'would probably even go with him for free!'

Nevertheless, by the time her shift was finished, she was so tired that she regretted promising Carlos that she would go home with him. But the deal was done and he was waiting for her outside the club. Natalia jumped into the shower, fighting her tiredness using an old and proven method – converting the amount she would make into *hryvni* and counting how many months it would take her to earn that money in Ukraine. That always worked. Fifteen minutes later they were catching a cab together on the dark and quiet street not far from our club.

Carlos's place was actually a small room in a lower-class apartment building that he was renting. It didn't even have its own toilet. There was only a sanitation unit that the entire floor used. The only furniture in his room was an old cupboard, a chair and a double bed.

'Disappointed, I thought to myself that semi-professional soccer doesn't pay that well, before taking up my duties…' continues Natalia, while sipping her drink.

'And there it started – the best sex I've ever had!' Her cheeks and ears are burning from the red wine and the memories of the passionate night. 'We did it for three hours, with short breaks to take a leak or smoke. It was so good that I even forgot that I was tired. And, I've been coming back since then almost every night after work, ignoring my exhaustion. For free! I even pay for the cab myself. Can you believe it?' finishes Natalia, with a contented smile on her face.

Lena and I nod, raising our eyebrows in surprise while ravenously chewing another piece of juicy sushi.

'Nothing wrong with that, Nata. It's called love! When two halves that are meant to be together, meet each other!' exclaims my middle sister, and my eyebrows rise even higher. 'I wonder what your children would look like ... they say that mixed-race kids are very beautiful!'

Natalia starts choking, from the wasabi or most probably from what she'd heard. 'Bite your tongue, Lena! It amazes me how quickly you turn everything into a serious relationship!'

'Okay. I agree. I may be a bit too much of a romantic person. But you cannot deny the fact that that's a woman's purpose – to reproduce and continue the human race. And for that she needs to find a good man, marry him and give him beautiful children ...'

'Yeah, right! Stay at home, cook, clean up and wash his socks while he is fucking around with other women like us. How many of the men who come to the clubs are married? Your concept of life is a bit out of date, my dear sister. You've got to wake up. A woman is not a thing that has a purpose! She, like any other creature on this planet, is born to enjoy life, to be free and happy. People like you also think that a cow has a purpose of supplying humankind with milk for as long as it lives. You are wrong! They are only supposed to produce milk to feed their babies, like any other mother does, including humans. Things like coffee machines and hairdryers have a purpose. The first makes coffee, the second helps to keep you prettier. But don't tell me that I was born with the purpose of getting married and becoming a baby-making machine!'

I stop eating and look at Natalia. Cows? Machines? Did I miss something? How did we get here?

The deeper my sister gets into the philosophy of life, the more emotional she becomes. Her sparkly eyes stand out starkly against her reddened face, and her intense gesticulations bring a lot of passion into her speech.

Lena is looking down into her plate. I can see the shade of regret of starting this conversation on her face. It's time for me to break into my sisters' discussion. I really don't feel like listening to the theory of why we come into this world for the rest of the lunch, and throw in the first thing that comes to my mind.

'And how big is his penis, Nata? I've heard black guys have huge ...' I say, with my mouth full of rice and fish.

Without even changing her pontifical tone, my elder sister jumps straight from women's predestination to the sizes of men's genitals.

'It's definitely bigger than normal … at least of all the ones I'd seen so far.' She looks at me, smiles and adds, softening her voice, 'You want to change the subject, Jul? Fine! But I don't want to talk about Carlos either – too much attention for just a fuck buddy. How is it going with Michel, Lena?'

'Oh, it's going great! He sent me a huge bunch of roses the other day, without any particular reason – how romantic is that? And he is taking me out for dinner to a very fancy restaurant tonight!' She is radiant with happiness. 'He is young and handsome with a good job; he treats me well. And on top of that, he told me that he loves children. I think he is The One for me …'

'Here we go again …' sighs Natalia. 'The fact that he loves children doesn't mean that he wants to have them, and especially, it doesn't mean that he wants to have them with you.' She starts getting agitated again. 'And I'm not saying it to upset you, Len. I just don't want you to amplify Michel's words with your imagination or fantasy. What I mean is, try to see the direct meaning of the words without adding anything to them. It will prevent you from being hurt in life. The problem with most women, including you, is that you draw your perfect picture, meet a man and then, by putting your meaning into his words, try to fit him into your picture, which usually makes your life more complicated. And even if he did say that he wanted to have children with you, it wouldn't necessarily mean that he meant it, which brings us to another conclusion – don't listen to his words. Look at his actions. The two unfortunately don't always match.'

I nod. Even though it's not pleasant to watch Lena's happy face turn sour, I add, 'Natalia has a point.'

But Lena doesn't want to give up and exclaims to Natalia, 'You are such a cynic! You cannot assume that all people around you are motivated by selfishness. We must think that all people are good unless proven otherwise.'

It is funny, but I nod again. I hold myself back from saying that Lena has a point too. I decide to stay out of it; it doesn't look like I am going to help to stop the argument, anyway.

To my surprise, Natalia just smiles and very calmly replies, 'I am a realist, Lena, А Это, как говорят в Одессе, две большие разницы[11]'.

Natalia had done this so many times before – tried to change Lena's way of seeing things in life – but it had never really worked and, as all three of us know, is not going to work this time either.

'Anyway, I am very glad that it's going well with you two, Lena. Just please try to take it easy this time …'

---

11 Russian, 'And as they say in Odessa, they are two huge differences.'

'I'll do my best, I promise!' smiles Lena and winks at us. 'Now it's your turn, Jul. What's new in your life since I last saw you?'

'Nothing much, if we're talking about my private life,' I answer after a short pause. 'Thanks to you, Nata, I'm so busy with the day shift freaks in the club that I don't have any desire to see them in my free time … unless I'm getting paid for it, of course.'

I take a long, deep drag of my cigarette, and watch the smoke I slowly blow out of my mouth. 'One thing I know for sure is that when I leave this place, there are going to be two things I'll never be able to enjoy ever again – men and champagne. I swear, if I ever had to meet the motherfucker who invented this whole getting-paid-for-drinking system, I would punch him in his face. Last night I had to carry Monica upstairs again! Can you believe it? Loaded, she passed out right on the client! They must either put in an elevator or get a bouncer to carry the drunken bitches upstairs. I'm sick and tired of it!'

The rest of our Sunday meeting we spend chatting about how sick and toxic the club system is. It is normal at the end of a night for some girls to be unable to walk up the stairs without help. But the problem isn't the absence of the lift or the bouncer, and we all know that. The problem is that nobody in the club – owner, manager, barman or clients – cares about the girls' health. They would watch you drink yourself to death, as long as they make their profit and have fun.

Champagne bar? Champagne slaughterhouse, more like it.

18

After lunch with my sisters, I go to a nightclub. As always on Sundays, the crowd consists mainly of my colleagues. All cabarets are closed on the holy day, and it is the only night for the girls to party. There are also a lot of clients in the crowd. Mostly jerks and assholes. The ones that never spend money on champagne during our working hours, brushing us off with 'not today … I am so tired … maybe next time' bullshit. However, when the acquaintance with the girl 'accidentally' takes place outside of the cabaret, they turn into pesky mosquitos, that all of a sudden are full of enthusiasm, hoping to get the romance for free.

God! I hate these cheap bastards!

Even though the DJ is rocking it and I've had a good amount of tequila and coke, I can't get into a clubbing mood. Every now and then one of these insects comes close with a stupid 'What is your name?' or 'Where are you from?', dragging me out of my flying-high-with-the-music state. I boldly put an irritated expression on my face, turn away and continue dancing. I don't even bother to respond.

I go back to the bar, order tequila, and start raiding my purse for money.

'Don't worry. I'll get it.'

I look up. He is tall, handsome, in his mid-thirties. His perfect grey suit accentuates his macho body type. And I don't remember seeing him before. Most likely he is not one of the regulars of our 'establishments'; at least he's missing that degenerate look in his eyes ...

... Oh my fuck ... his charming blue eyes ... hmm ...

He signals to the barman, who without delay starts carrying out the silent order. Then he turns back to me with a naughty smile, 'I have an indecent proposal for you ...'

I lift my eyebrows – that is an unusual pick-up line. He's got my full attention.

'I am here with my girlfriend,' he nods towards the VIP section. 'She finds you very attractive,' and after a quick pause with a charming twinkle, 'and so do I, of course ... Sometimes we like to have a little bit of fun, and tonight, we would love you to join us …'

'I don't do girls,' I throw, turn to the bar counter, and pointedly pay for my drink.

He bursts into laughter and steps close to me, giving me no other choice but to shift back and face him. He is so close that our lips almost touch and I sense the strength of his body. The wave of tempting lust surprisingly drinks me in.

Hmmm … those blue eyes …

'Let's have some fun … I am sure you wouldn't mind doing me, would you?' His body language screams arrogant confidence but his face is full of genuine excitement.

The barman puts a bottle of Dom Perignon and two glasses in front of him. 'Anything else, Mr. Harvey?' Without taking his naughty look off me, he replies, 'Bring me a third glass. This pretty lady is going to join us.'

Hmmm … Harvey? You've got it all … including your bloody girlfriend …

She is a beautiful, well-groomed, young and extremely sweet girl. 'Hi, my name is Katherine,' she greets, as if we had been best friends all our lives.

The night is flowing fabulously. We drink, sniff, dance and laugh like crazy.

Then, my new friends suggest that I continue the party in their suite. They are staying in some luxury boutique hotel, five minutes away from the disco club. I seriously doubt the proposal, but their story about the generous mountain of coke they left in the room doesn't really leave me a choice.

As we walk in, Harvey heads straight to the coffee table, elegantly drops onto the chair and picks up the phone.

'Bring us two bottles of Cristal and ice please. *Merci.*'

He hangs up and lights a cigarette.

Katherine playfully grins, 'Let's blow his mind away …' and pulls me into the bathroom.

It's a spacious, white marble room with two basins, a huge shower and a stunning free-standing tub. She switches on the water in the shower, intriguingly smiles and presses the button next to the light switch. A white blind starts rising, surprisingly unveiling the show window, which is the wall between the bedroom and the bathroom.

Oh wow … he is going to watch us doing it … this is mind-blowing!

Katherine quickly drops her clothes onto the floor, steps under the stream and playfully beckons to me. I follow her steps. We soap each other and kiss while slowly rubbing with white foam every part of our bodies. Her knowing hands are playing with my clit. The hot flow pleasantly strikes my neck and shoulders, while she sucks and bites my nipples.

She is good … it's all so unexpectedly good …

She turns me around, puts both of my hands on the glass and starts fingering my pussy from behind. Her other hand wanders between my neck and my breasts. I roll my eyes in pre-orgasmic rapture and don't even notice that the room service guy is here.

The young man hurriedly places the cart-table and the shiny ice bucket with two golden necks sticking out of it, opens one of the bottles, gets Harvey to sign a check and leaves the room while demonstratively looking away from the window. But I don't care ... neither does Katherine ... she doesn't stop until I come ...

... I open my eyes. I am in my bed.

I have a horrible hangover and cannot really understand if last night was a drunken dream or a stoned reality.

I reach to my side table to get some aspirin and bump my purse. I open it and find €1,000 and a note:

I took the liberty and hope I didn't offend you. You were so pleasant and tasty ☺. *I just wanted to show my appreciation and this is the best way I know ... Thank you, Julia.*

H.

The memories of last night fragmentally begin to come back. His greedy lips ... his strong and wide shoulders ... his attentive and demanding hands ... his swollen and pulsating ...

Hmmm Harvey, Harvey ... you are not just a good lover but a gentleman too ... I wish you had it all but your bloody girlfriend!

19

It is Monday. The shift is quiet – no more than we expect it to be. In the first hour, there are no customers at all, then one or two useless Coca-Cola regulars arrive. As always, they just sip the virulent brown liquid and stare at the big screen's perverted porn. The girls and I kill the first two hours chatting. As we cover all the latest news that is travelling around the cabarets, some juicy gossip from around the world, and even the current weather conditions in Ukraine and Russia and how they are influencing the wheat crop, Death shows up.

The procedure of his visit remains the same; he hobbles to the bar table, where the barman enthusiastically greets him and pours his usual soda.

Of course he greets enthusiastically – it's not his job to go with the oldie upstairs! His job is the easy one – just opening the fucking bottle. God, I hate them all!

A few minutes later, the manager comes out of his office and they start their casual chit-chat, which all the girls know will end up with the manager recommending one of the girls and Death choosing his next victim.

We also all know that there is only one person in this place who is not aware of what is happening, and it is a new girl. A moment later, the manager calls her and the three of them go upstairs.

All the girls including me sigh with relief, and go on with our usual talk about how the new girl is going to take her baptism of fire, and how nice it would be if Death kicked the bucket and went in peace forever. And if he did, and it happened while he was upstairs, would the police close down the cabaret and investigate? For how many days would it stay closed?

Our 'innocent' conversation doesn't last for long. Ten minutes later the new girl, covered with tears and snot, runs down the stairs straight to the bathroom. The manager comes down too, looks around and waves to me, indicating that I have to take up the new girl's duties.

Oh, crap!

On the way up, I keep wondering which is worse: to go there for the first time and learn, one by one, each of the disgusting things that will happen, or to go there as I am, fully aware of what is about to come next.

In the middle of my dilemma I enter the private room. This time, for some reason, the manager has taken him to the VIP *séparé* that has a shower in it and a free-standing leather couch right in the centre of the room. Death is sitting on the couch, already naked but observing proprieties by being covered with his white undershirt. There is a striking indignation and dissatisfaction on his face.

You old bastard, you actually think someone could enjoy this?

I join him on the couch. Deeply and morbidly I breathe in, thinking to myself that if I've done it once I can do it again. I breathe out, smile and come out with, 'Hey sexy! What's up?'

You know what happens for the next hour; I am sure you don't need a reminder, and I am trying hard to think about these moments as little as possible.

As soon as we finish, I pick him up from the couch to help him to get dressed. He is so weak that he loses his balance and leans against the couch, which is fucking free-standing! The leather seat slides away and Death falls onto the floor. I try to pick him up, but can't. There is nothing in the room that we can use as a point of support except the walls, which are not an option because Death is stretched out right in the middle of the room. I rush to the door to call somebody to help, but grandpa stops me. He explains that he doesn't want anybody to see him naked and helpless on the floor. I nod, go back to him, and before trying to get him back on his feet, take off my killer 21 cm heels.

Smart girl! What can I say ...

After a few more attempts, I finally pull him back onto the couch. We catch our breath and then dress. Before leaving, Death shoves a €50 note into my hand with the words, 'You are a good girl, Julia.' I take the money, say thanks and wish never to see this man again, even if it means that he has to give up the ghost for it.

20

The next day, the shift is even worse. Normally trade picks up towards the weekend, but not this week. I am glad that at least I made a bottle yesterday, because it looks like for most of the girls, it will be a second day in a row with zero.

Just before the end of the shift, I manage to convince one weirdo to buy me a *demi-bouteille* for a hand-job in a semi-private lounge. As soon as we get comfortable and the barman opens the bottle, I reach to open the zip of his pants, but he stops me, turns my face to his and passionately asks, 'Kiss me first, please.'

The case is well dressed, about fifty years old, not too ugly or repulsive. But there is a strange – I would even say maniacal – shade in his eyes.

I answer 'Sure,' and let him kiss me on the lips.

Here we go again! What's wrong with all these men?

Once again, he just sticks his wet and slimy tongue down my throat and forces it around, trying to get as deep as possible for a couple of minutes.

How someone can even call that a kiss? Yuck!

Then he pushes me away, holding my shoulders firmly, and says, 'Please come with me tonight. I will pay you €300 for the night.'

Oh my fuck! Another nutcase …

There is no way I am going out with him – especially since I already have four regulars. They are my constant income from my out-of-the-club activities that keep me quite busy …

One of them is a Jewish lawyer whose abnormality is his absolute normality. He is not an attractive or a generous man at all, but he loves good food, treats me with respect and his knowledge of sex doesn't reach beyond the missionary position. Another one is from Belgium. This guy loves to go to restaurants and guzzle like it is the last day of his life. He always jokes loudly about sex and how good he is at it, despite having an extra-small dick that is generously shaded by his big belly, making him the perfect candidate for the Dickie Do Award 4XL T-shirt. On top of this, he laughs pathetically every time he ejaculates. Then there is a German guy, one of the most normal men I've met in Luxembourg: a good fuck, but absolutely unemotional. And another regular is a Portuguese guy. A nice fellow, but with some shortcomings as well – he comes too quickly. I feel sorry for him and always try to move more slowly and less intensely, making sure that the intercourse and his pleasure lasts longer, but our record is 4 minutes and 10 seconds from the moment I unzip his pants.

In other words, I definitely have enough of a bizarre clientele in my after-work life!

I am free as a bird tonight, seeing none of my regulars, but I shake my head and say, 'Can't do it, I am busy tonight.'

The nutcase takes my hands in his and passionately responds, 'Please, Julia, I will give you €500! Please come with me tonight!'

Seriously ... how can I say no to €500! So what if he is a creep?

At the end of my shift, my new case is waiting for me in a cab. As soon as I jump in, he tells the driver his address and we leave.

It is close to 11 p.m. already and in the darkness, I don't follow where we are going. The area we arrive at looks decent; he stays on the third floor of the four-storey apartment building. It all seems good until we walk into his place. It is a studio stuffed with rubbish and old junk. It is so cluttered that there is no space even to sit on his only couch. The smell inside is so intense: a mixture of naphthalene, dirt and staleness. Screw the money – I will not be able to spend the night in here.

I quickly look at my phone, fake concern on my face, apologise and explain that for some unforeseen reason I can't stay the whole night, and that if he wants to, we can do a quickie for half the price and then I have to leave.

He looks upset, but he nods with understanding and offers me a glass of wine in the meantime.

I agree that this is a great idea. As soon as we clink our glasses, I drain mine. The alcohol relaxes me right away, but some time later I start feeling heaviness and drowsiness too.

I wake up in the morning, naked in his bed, covered with smelly and dirty sheets. The bastard must have drugged me. I quickly get out of the bed, still feeling dizzy, and find my clothes hanging on the chair. While I am hurriedly dressing, I try to remember what happened last night and think what I'm going to do next.

The sound of the toilet flushing frightens me. I turn towards the bathroom and there he is, standing in his boxers and socks. The pathetic motherfucker smiles at me as if nothing had happened, and serenely says, 'Good morning, beautiful. Would you like some coffee?'

The sound of his absorbing voice sparks some memories of last night: him taking me to the bed, me still sluggishly objecting, but already unable to move my hands. I remember him kissing, grabbing and fucking me dazed and unconscious, and how he kept repeating maniacally, 'I know you love me, I know you do ...'

The vivid recollection punches through me like an electric shock.

I don't even put my shoes on, just grab them with my bag and back up towards the door.

As soon as I touch the handle of the door, I freak out, 'Where is my money? You haven't paid me, you sick bastard!'

The look in his eyes changes from dull-innocent to reptilian-mean, but his voice stays the same.

'Sorry, beautiful, but I don't have the money. Come, have some coffee with me, my love.'

I storm out of that place, down the stairs to the street, and run until I see a cab that is driving past. I wave to stop it, climb in, tell the driver the address of the club and then just start crying ...

My anger and resentment for the dickhead as well as for myself rend me into pieces. I can't stop my tears, even when the cab driver starts giving me discontented looks in the mirror. No matter how much I hate the prick, I know it's my fault. I dragged myself into this situation ...

I decide not to tell anybody. I am too ashamed to talk about it. I have to try to forget it. It never happened to me.

21

It is the end of another working shift. I had very satisfying trading – went upstairs twice, plus a few *piccolos* at the bar – so I'm slightly smashed. Besides, I sniffed some in the toilet with Margo, the only girl I have something in common with, of all the girls on the day shift. We are quite spaced out and are having a jolly chat at the bar when this guy walks in.

Margo recognises him on the spot, but oddly turns away and starts looking attentively at her nails, pretending that she hasn't noticed him. I point the man out with my eyebrows and nudge her with my elbow, asking if she is going to work. In response, without taking her gaze off her hand, she snaps 'I don't feel like working; he is yours.' The fermentation never makes me extra suspicious, but the enigma of why Margo, who hasn't made any money today, gives up the opportunity so easily, does not bother me at all. Plus the buzz is great. Without any hesitation I jump off the bar stool and slide towards the man.

He is a droll character: short, plumpish, with a James Bond attitude. His pants, jacket, and even his cowboy hat are made of black leather.

I wonder how many poor animals had to die for him to dress today.

He really looks funny, and it takes an effort not to show the amusement on my face. Instead I cover my face with an oh-you-are-so-cool-and-sexy look, and whisper a seductive hello. He looks at me without any enthusiasm, then turns back to his gin and tonic without acknowledging me.

Normally this type of attitude drives me mad. I start to freak out, and most times just leave the rude bastard – but because my successful day has kicked my mood up, I decide to try again. I draw very close, pressing my body against his shoulder, then slowly but firmly grab his bull neck while tickling it with my nails, and whisper in his ear, 'You wanna fuck?'

He turns to me again. I pierce him with my signature smoky come-to-bed look and add a come-hither-I-am-so-horny smile.

The left corner of his mouth curves, indicating a smile. He looks me over, as if I am a sweatshirt he is about to buy in the shop, and says, 'Okay. You asked for it,' before rushing towards the stairs.

That was an easy one. Margo would kick herself if she knew how quickly I arranged my third bottle.

The rest is supposed to be a piece of cake: quickly screw the cowboy and fuck off home, maybe even go to celebrate my highly fertile shift with a few hits in a nightclub.

When the champagne is served and the *garçon* leaves, the roly-poly unbuttons his jacket, pulls some stuff out of the inner pockets and places them on the table. The stuff includes metal serrated and chained nipple clips, a few rubbers, a tube of anal lubricant and a bottle of poppers[12].

I swallow a glass of bubbly and sigh. Even though I am heavily intoxicated, it is not difficult for me to imagine the full version of what is about to happen if my *vaquero* is going to use all these items on me. Especially considering that I am an anal virgin, and that just the idea of somebody sticking something up my ass seriously freaks me out. And my nipples, although they have a boyish look, are quite sensitive.

What can I say? It looks like I am in deep shit again.

He looks at me with a smile, as if he reads my mind: 'Those are for me, but if you want to try them,

12 Poppers: a slang term for alkyl nitrites that are often inhaled to enhance sexual pleasure

you are welcome.' I also smile – with relief – and mumble, 'No thank you.'

He liberates himself from his tiring outfit and throws my dress down to the floor. For some time we just kiss while he squeezes my thighs and digs my slit with his fingers. I palm his dick and rub it down, but it is still soft.

He attaches the clips to his nipples, picks up the poppers and makes himself comfortable lying on his right side, leaning on the armrest, with his legs spread wide. He grips the back of my neck, presses my face to his hips, and sniffs from the little bottle. His body reacts immediately and his cock swells and stiffens in my mouth.

Damn, this shit smells terrible.

The erection doesn't last long; just a minute or two. As soon as his penis softens again, he picks up the lubricant and condoms from the table and goes back to his relaxed position. He orders me to go down on the floor on my knees, sniffs again and pushes his solidifying cock to the back of my throat.

A few minutes later, my kinky cowboy unpacks a condom. Instead of putting it on his penis, he grasps my hand, straightens my fingers and unrolls it over them, stretching the rubber down my wrist. Then he squeezes some lube onto the condom, draws in some more of the smelly shit and orders, 'Put it in,' while placing my hand at his bunghole.

Unfuckingbelievable – my horseman turns out to be headless for real!

My mind boggles for a moment but I push my hand in. *Whatever! As long as he doesn't encroach on my ass.* When all my fingers drown inside him, he takes my hand and pushes it further, until it disappears up to my wrist.

'Crook your fingers inside,' he orders again with ease. I peep at him. His face is ridiculously delighted. I cannot see my hand but I visualise my long nails that will scratch him inside and shake my head. He sniffs some more and smiles. 'Don't worry, doll. Just do it. Make a fist.'

The rest of our hour-long session I anal-intrude him while enthusiastically sucking his cock, helping with my left hand to maintain its hardness. When eventually he comes loudly, I remove my hand. It's covered with blood. I roll off the condom and hurriedly wipe the remains of the red stains off my hands. I fight the strong urge to vomit, quickly dress without saying a word, and rush out of the room. But I realise that I will never make it to the bathroom, come back and puke right into the champagne bucket.

* * *

The rest is a haze. The next thing I remember, I am in the middle of the club sitting on top of Margo, on the floor, kicking her and pulling her hair.

She knew. She didn't tell me.

The night shift is already here. When I turn to dodge Margo's attempt to slap me, I spot Natalia's distorted face above me. It looks like she is trying to shout something at me, but no words are coming out. Like somebody has turned the volume down. All I can hear is humming noises.

Natalia is trying to drag me off Margo, but the rage makes me surprisingly strong. I brush her away while slapping and scratching my victim underneath me.

'Jul, stop it! Jul! If I told you, he would have never taken you! This prick's main thrill is to stun and sicken the girl!' Margo keeps uttering but I can't hear her either.

Unfuckingbelievable how booze so easily transforms some people from normal to angry, strong and absolutely stupid creatures ...

Apparently, we make so much noise that even the boss steps out of his office to check what's happening. He estimates the amount of damage and calmly tells Natalia, 'Get your fucking sister out of here or I will fire her.' When he sees that I am totally stoned and out of control, he grabs a jug from the bar and splashes me with ice-cold water.

I freeze. Margo fizzles, removes me – setting herself free, she throws 'Crazy bitch!' at me and leaves the club.

Without taking his sinister eyes off me, the boss shouts, 'Stop staring and go back to work, people.' He turns to Natalia. 'With all my love to you, Princess, next month this junkie is out of my club.'

22

The next few days I spend in bed – I call in sick and don't show up at work. Four months of being deeply soaked in booze, stress and perverted extremes have exhausted my nerves. I haven't been able to eat anything for three days – my memory won't let go of the bright images of my adventure with the cowboy, which has wiped out my appetite. The only substance that enters my body is the fume of the burned cannabis plant.

Someone knocks on the door. It can't be Masha. She went for lunch with some customer from last night *(the poor guy probably didn't notice an Adam's apple in the darkness of the club).* Besides, she knows the door is not locked.

'Go away! Nobody is home!'

I turn away from the door and pull the blanket over my head.

'If nobody is home, who is speaking, then?' laughs Lena and lets herself in. She walks through the dark room, flings open the curtains and continues, 'Jul, what's happening? Aren't you going to Natalia's birthday dinner?'

Crap, I completely forgot about it!

'I don't feel well, I can't ...' I mumble, burying myself even deeper under the blanket while making my voice sound sick.

Damn, why didn't I lock the door?

Lena comes to the bed, peels the blanket off me and chatters, 'You are definitely going to get worse if you don't go out and get some fresh air. Look at you! Nothing but bones. You must eat something! We are doing Italian today, seems like a good place. Get up now, dress and put a smile on your face.'

I know there is only one way to keep her quiet ...

I pull on the sweater and jeans that are the first things to come into my hands, ignoring Lena's telling-off that I must dress up because we are going to a restaurant. I brush my eyelashes with mascara a few times, grab a jacket.

'I'm ready. Let's stop at the florist first.'

I'm surprised to see Margo at the table, next to Natalia. I stop indecisively, holding the flowers. Margo smiles at me.

'Oh, stop it, Jul. I've already forgotten about it. If I were in your place, I probably would have lost it too. I should have warned you anyway.'

When, finally, I find the strength to look her in the eye, I notice a few scratches on her cheek.

'Was that me? Sorry, Margo, I didn't mean to …'

Natalia takes my hand, and pulls me down to sit. Then she takes the flowers.

'Thanks Jul. They are lovely.'

We order drinks, make the first toast for the birthday girl. The conversation flows and the evening is pleasant.

Natalia tells us about her idea of how to invest our money when we get back to Ukraine, reminding Lena how pointlessly they blew their earnings after their previous contract. The plan is simple – to put our money together and buy an apartment in Kiev. She has already found a flat through her friend, a realtor. The owners are chronic alcoholics, and desperately need money to pay some debts, so they are not asking for much. Her friend promises to hold it for another two months, knowing that Natalia is a cash buyer. They bargained and met at 55 grand US, a fantastic price for a three-bedroom apartment close to the center of Kiev. 'We could pool together and buy it!' finishes Natalia, with a spark of excitement and confidence in her eyes.

'We could renovate it and maybe rent it out!' exclaims Lena, and we all nod in agreement.

'It sounds so cool! Now I am jealous. I wish I could go in with you, dolls, but I've already promised my brother I'd help him with his businesses,' Margo sighs and pouts.

The food is delicious. We order more wine. We talk and laugh a lot. Oh … I've missed these always-fun times with my sisters.

When we move on to dessert, Natalia looks at me with a slight touch of worry and asks, 'Where are you planning to work next month?'

I shrug. 'I have no idea …'

'Well, I have a few places in mind. Would you like me to check it out for you?'

'Oh, Nata, what would I do without you …' I move closer to hug her and realise that my eyes have filled with hot tears. 'Thank you so much …'

Damn! When did I become this emotional?

'No worries, you know I love you, my Poppy-seed, so much, and would do anything for you …' she says while hugging me back.

Without any hesitation, Lena sprinkles with tears too, through her happy smile, and locks us in her arms. 'I love you both so much too!'

Margo turns red. 'Dolls, stop this drama right now! People are staring, and I look like an idiot now, here alone.'

Then, 'Oh ... what the hell!' she says, moves closer and hugs us too. 'I love you too, my crazy bitches!'

And we laugh again ...

23

The rest of the time in Luxenbourg I spend like a hamster in a wheel – I work in a peep show.

This is a place where the client enters one of eight small cabins, which frame the round, non-stop rotating stage, called a drum. He drops a €2 coin into the box and the viewing window opens onto the drum, for a few minutes, while the performer does a striptease show. The explicitness of the dancer teases the spectator, while the dark cabin and paper towels suggest relief through self-stimulation – in other words, jerking off.

A few days after the birthday party, Natalia victoriously walked into my room and said that she'd found the club for me. I felt relief, but only until it was announced it was a peep show. Her scrambled explanation of what it was and why she couldn't find me a normal cabaret shocked me.

'Jul, the upside is that you don't have to cram yourself with bubbly every day ... it's an even better option!'

No shit! A better option?!

The idea of revealing my fanny in public repelled me ... It is one thing to dance on the stage, at least three meters away from the clients, and take your panties off to the final chords of the song, while modestly keeping your legs crossed. The peep show is a completely different story. It is a gynecologist's room where, besides the doctor, there are another seven freaks with affectionate interest staring at your pussy ...

Why? Why? Why Nata? Why did you do it to me?

There are five girls besides me working here: one Ukrainian and four from Hungary. It takes me by surprise, because I never saw or heard of any Western European girls working in the cabarets. Why, then, the peep show? It's a place that all the girls, including me and my compatriot and new colleague, Vlada, are scared of and scorn as a shameful honky-tonk. It takes me some time to answer.

It's simple. All the girls dance on the drum, one after another, for four minutes each; so, we have a 20-minute break between our turns, which we spend in the waiting room with couches and a TV, a small kitchen with a fridge, and a shower. The working shift is long – twelve hours. So, we are allowed a one-hour break during the day.

Besides the systematic performing, we also give private shows in a separate cabin, which is a small room with only two chairs facing each other, separated by a glass wall. If a client likes a dancer on the drum, he can call her for a private show – €30 for ten minutes, of which €10 goes to the club and €20 to the girl. Besides that, there is a salary, which is an equal share between the girls and the owner from the €2 coin collection. In the private cabin, everything is allowed with only one restriction – the invisible barrier between the participants.

At first, I am bogged down in denial, fed by my complexes and fears.

This place is nothing but a sick zoo. I will linger here for a month and then Natalia will help me to find another cabaret.

While our pride makes Vlada and me cover our pussies on the drum, and we don't get even one private dance the entire week, the Hungarian girls manage to do up to ten private shows every day, sometimes even more. Each time they pass by and glance over at our Ukrainian-cheerless couch while rushing to their next private dance, they wear these half-pity-half-snooty smiles on their faces.

Dirty sluts!

Okay, it takes me some time, but eventually I get the picture ... the Hungarians are making the same money as we do in a cabaret. Probably even more, not only without sexual intercourse or even a single touch, but also without drinking their asses to death while someone fucks their vaginas and brains. (As we already know, 99 per cent of the cabarets' clients first bonk the entertainer's cerebrum before they decide to buy the bubbly; then, if she is lucky and the expenditure is done, her pussy too.) Here, any kind of contact is excluded, except for visual communication.

Yeah, I know ... I'm slow, and could have made this scientific breakthrough on my first working day! I probably shouldn't smoke pot ...

So while we Eastern Europeans think that the peep show is a vulgar and dirty place to work, the smart women, like the Hungarians, are squeamish about champagne bars and actually have a very well paid and germ-free job.

I start watching them. They use different wigs, and often choose some accessories for the costumes, like a policeman's hat, French maid's apron or kinky collars and handcuffs – and, more importantly, sex toys too. They'll do anything but be modest or conventional. They are not ashamed of opening their legs wide or coming loud, while getting carried away by self-stimulation on the drum or in a private room.

Eventually, I get tired of it. Someone is constantly making money in front of my face while I bitch and moan and keep my net sales miserably low. First, I visit a local sex shop and buy some seductive lingerie, lubricant, one small-to-medium-sized vibrator, and another black, considerably sized dildo.

I don't even know if I am going to use it, but the satisfier looks so naughty that I can't resist ...

My new purchases help immediately – I am called for a few private dances and get some appraising looks from the Hungarian girls.

Still, there is a huge difference between my earnings and the Hungarian girls'. I decide to fight my shame and open up my legs more, so the men can properly see my moist, pinkish slit. As a result, my sales increase by 20 per cent and Vlada stops talking to me.

But when I begin to relax totally on the drum and enjoy myself – I'm talking about self-stimulation with, sometimes, a happy ending – my income jumps by another 50 per cent. And with time, I even manage to score a few regular customers – potential paedophiles who love my extra-small body size and flat chest.

Since starting the peep show I feel like a cosmonaut who is getting ready for a moon landing. Twelve hours a day, every 20 minutes, the same routine and movement while turning on the drum ... over and over. It's like the movie *Groundhog Day*. The constant rotation makes me nauseous and dizzy. After my shift I climb into bed and close my eyes, but my head is still spinning, making me feel sick. I even end up throwing up, until a few days ago one of the Hungarians took pity on me and advised me to get some pills, which helped at least to take the spinning-in-bed symptoms away.

The constant repetition and the long working hours don't help me to keep my spirits up. In moments of deep self-pity, and with a strong desire to break the cycle and walk away, I remind myself about one customer I had while working the day shift in Sexy Girls …

He was about 60, tall and thin, and worked as an auto mechanic. His hands were always dirty; he smelled of sweat, as if he'd never been in the shower; and his mouth had a set of yellow stinky teeth, which often smirked on his badly dented and tanned face. He always ordered one regular Coke and stared at the big screen, covered by constantly moving genitalia. If I was really persistent, in exchange for a *piccolo* and right by the bar, he would dig my pussy with his two fingers, scratching it with his nails, under my skirt, so nobody around would notice …

These revolting, vivid images always help me to appreciate what I have – no, what I *don't* have – to deal with while working at the peep show!

24

There are plenty of upsides to this new, unusual employment *(yeah, as if drinking and fucking some freaks is a usual kind of job)*, especially my relative sobriety.

I don't drink, and have stopped going out after work, because the long hours and the stress of all the exercise make me quite disciplined. I've forgotten when I last used heavy drugs, including cocaine. The only reward that I allow myself is the joint that I draw on every night while lying in bed (I was lucky to get a tiny, cupboard-sized room with space for only one bed, so I don't have any roommates to complain about the smoke), with the lights off, watching the smoke curling through the street glow, melting in my happy – *oh, and usually very coherent* – place.

I have another pleasant surprise when I work out how much money I've made, considering my absolutely useless beginning. In three weeks I made the same amount as I made in the cabaret in a full month. Without a doubt, I decide to stay at the peep show for the next month, and am really looking forward to seeing how much I can make using all my newly acquired tricks and skills together with my open-minded attitude.

I even find a fun part of my occupation – watching the customers, discovering how freaky the freaks can be – and wonder at the certainty that I will never stop wondering.

Except for one incident, when I ended up puking in the toilet because of one degenerate client: while masturbating, he bent over, slid his asshole apart, scraped the shit out of it using four fingers, ate it off his palm, ejaculated into the same hand, then polished the cum off like it was a delicious topping to the brownie he'd just eaten …

Yuck! I still cannot forgive myself for not turning my face away or just closing my eyes and protecting my future life from these disgusting memories that keep on flashing through my head.

Generally, the weirdos don't bother me. I do what I have to do: play sexy, climax once in a while and keep observing the pure deviation.

The guys like Lena's new adorer, who likes to wear women's stockings, don't bowl me over any more.

Ha! Red stockings …? How about the pink G-string on the big, muscular guy who looks like the Commando starred by Arnold Schwarzenegger that can literally hold only one of his balls? Or the full set of white and lacy lingerie, including bra, and the pre-staged game in which the dude bends over the chair assuming the doggy position with his back to me while I menacingly shout at him, 'You dirty, little bitch! I am going to nail you right now …' while he frantically masturbates until he discharges, enjoying his humiliation.

Then there's this other nutcase who masturbates without touching his tool. He takes his pants off, unbuttons his shirt and lifts his arms behind his head. He starts moving his body, violently throwing his penis against his stomach and hips. Um … how can I describe it? Imagine your garden hose, with the water turned to full pressure, that you've accidently dropped on the ground. Vivid, isn't it? The extrovert whips himself with his own dick until he comes, while I play with myself, watch him, and pretend that I am extremely turned on by his routine.

Also, there is a Russian guy, Ruslan. He is one of a kind, as well. When he called me to the private cabin, he asked me not to take my clothes off and to do nothing but simply talk to him.

Yeah, can you believe it? That's never happened to me before!

He hates cabarets, because, as he explains to me, 'Each time I've been to one I've ended up trying to escape from another drunk girl who'd got all upset and personal because I didn't want to sleep with her.'

It sounds suspicious. Why wouldn't he want to have some 'fun' instead of talking? I bet his tool is not working.

I keep these thoughts to myself. It's always better to get into the role of soul therapist than to rub my already tired and swollen pussy again.

The weirdos don't take me by surprise any more, but I still struggle to understand why handsome young guys would visit such places. There are quite few of them. And I am not talking about pimpled high-school students, or the poor perverts whose childhoods, taking into account Sigmund Freud's theory, I always tried to avoid imagining in order to preserve my mental well-being. I mean the guys in their late twenties or thirties, who definitely give the impression of some kind of success. Why would they come to a peep show in the first place? Why would they choose masturbation over sex, especially when they must have partners, given their fair looks and well-proportioned and functioning penises?

... Until, one day ...

I had a private session with a very handsome guy with a very handsome limb between his legs. When

I walked into the room, he stood right by the glass and asked me to do the same, holding me spellbound with his big, dark, far-reaching eyes. We were so close to each other that if there were no glass, we would feel the warmth of each other's bodies. His gaze was deep and provoking. A wave of lust suffocated my body. He asked me to take off my silky lace nightgown, slowly, while he softly breathed how beautiful I was and gently brushed the glass as he would my body. I stood with my legs spread shoulder-width. With one hand, I lightly rubbed my clit; with the other, I followed his hand's movement over the cold glass, caressing my flaming body. We both came at the same time.

I experienced a surprisingly powerful O, followed by the stream of hot tears that covered my face. As my body calmed down, my ecstasy became bitter sadness – one of my best sexual experiences had been sealed behind damn glass.

Interesting ... what we find weird or freaky in the beginning can sometimes turn out to be very sensual and enjoyable. It actually doesn't really matter why someone does this or that, as long as he or she finds pleasure in it without harming others.

Or maybe I'm totally turning into some kind of freak myself ...

25

I'm surprised when, a few days after my psychotherapy session with Ruslan, he comes back to see me.

He takes a private dance, as he did last time, and spends 10 minutes on casual chit-chat. He asks a lot about my family and me. How I've got to Luxembourg and how much longer I am going to stay in the country. He seems charming, funny and sweet. When our session is over and he gets up from the chair to leave, he stops at the door, and, overcoming his childish timidity, asks if I would like to join him for coffee sometime and takes my number.

He is shy to ask me out – so cute!

We start meeting for coffee almost every day before my shift, in the café across the road from the club. We laugh a lot, talk about life and our families, about our plans for the future, sharing even the most unrealistic, and that is why embarrassing and never-spoken-about dreams.

For me, the biggest attraction of our innocent attachment (besides, of course, that he is smart, handsome, always light-hearted, *and* speaks my native language) is that my new Russian friend is not trying to get under my skirt. Our relationship isn't going further than easy-going, joyful friendship and, sometimes, artless flirting.

I feel that I can relate to him. He also comes from nowhere and, just like us, he is trying to get out and have a decent life. Once, he shook me up with the fascinating and tragic story of his immigration from Russia to Europe, while he was still a teen-ager ...

His mother, Ayshe, was Chechen. She was born and lived in a small village a hundred kilometers from Groznyy. His father, Bashir, died from a stab wound during some stupid fight when Ruslan was only three. Ayshe loved Ruslan's father very much, and for a long time couldn't get over her loss. But when the tragic news reached them, her parents breathed a sigh of relief. Even though Bashir was a good man and husband, his temper was easily inflamed. They suspected that he'd eventually get himself into trouble, and worried that the trouble may one day involve Ayshe and Ruslan too.

When the first Chechen war started, Ruslan was fourteen years old. It was then that Ayshe met a Russian soldier, Sergey, whose battalion was stationed temporarily near Ayshe and Ruslan's village. The two fell in love at first sight. Their feelings were so strong that she ignored her parents' warnings to stop her 'outrageous sin' (obviously, a love affair with the enemy was a betrayal) before it was too late: no one knew how dangerous it could become if the villagers found out about it.

The romance between Ayshe and Sergey was intense but short. When the battalion eventually pulled out, all she was left with were her lover's promises that he'd come back against all odds, and the suspicious looks of her parents and neighbours when her belly started to grow. Was he killed, or was she just another trivial love story that he'd forgotten about as soon as he left with the troops? Time passed; he did not show up; Ruslan's mother couldn't keep her pregnancy a secret anymore.

Eventually she told her parents everything. They knew that she would not be able to stay safely in the village if she kept the child. But Ayshe refused an abortion, and they decided to send her and Ruslan to Groznyy, to their only relative, Aunt Fatima, for good.

It turned out that Fatima had some – as she called them – 'useful acquaintances', with whom she'd kept in contact for a rainy day. Luckily the old woman was kind, and without hesitation used her contacts to help Ayshe and Ruslan to escape to Moscow. There, they met with some more of Fatima's 'useful acquaintances', who helped to organise passports and refugee papers so that the two could immigrate to Europe.

The next few weeks were hell for fifteen-year-old Ruslan and pregnant Ayshe. Money was so tight that they had to change from buses to trains to hitch-hiking, almost starving every day. Ayshe's labour started in Ukraine, when they were about to enter Poland. Luckily they met a hauler who helped them through the border crossing without problems or delays, and then took them straight to the closest hospital.

But another tragedy awaited them. The baby boy was stillborn. As doctors tried to explain, it probably happened because of Ayshe's physical and emotional exhaustion. She was devastated. But she couldn't afford to collapse under this tragedy; she had to take care of Ruslan.

For the next year they wandered throughout Europe, from one low-paid job and homeless shelter to another. Until one day Ayshe met an old man somewhere in Germany, who was looking for a live-in housekeeper to do cleaning, cooking and grocery shopping. His wife had died a few months earlier and he couldn't cope on his own. He didn't mind Ayshe's son also staying with them, on condition that the boy went to school and spent his spare time helping around the house.

Things worked well until the old man started to intimidate the poor woman. First there were vulgar jokes and suggestions, then his harassment became more demanding and aggressive. The old man started threatening her: 'I will go to the police and report on you and your bastard son, and you will go to jail or be deported back to Russia.' He kept repeating it until Ayshe couldn't resist anymore and let the prick climb on top of her.

Ruslan couldn't understand why his mother cried at night, and why the lusty, satisfied smile wouldn't leave the old man's face. But it was not in his nature to question his mother and get involved in the adults' lives.

With time, Ayshe complied, for Ruslan's sake. She and the German even started living as husband and wife.

Five years later she died of cancer. Ruslan left the house and never saw the man again.

He moved to Luxembourg, where he found a job at an IT company. In just a few years he progressed from being a clerk to a programmer.

My heart bled listening to that. The image of the boy who'd been through more at his young age than most people had experienced in a lifetime, tore me apart.

I hugged him tightly. 'It's all good now … it's all behind you. You were a very brave little boy who's grown into a not-so-smart but very handsome man,' I teased Ruslan, and his face brightened with a smile.

26

It is the last week of our trip and I am busy packing. It turns out I've bought too many clothes and shoes during these six months. *Damn shopping therapy.* Half of my stuff doesn't fit into my bags; I have to mail a few extra boxes to Ukraine. I'm doing all of these chores – including buying souvenirs for our family and a few friends, having goodbye lunches with some of my regular clients, and, most important, going to the post office to draw all the money I've made – with a great thrill and an irrepressible smile on my face.

Yay! I am going home!

I take off the night before my departure. Ruslan invites me to his favorite Italian restaurant. I look forward to a pleasant night with the person to whom, in just a couple of weeks, I have got so attached, even more so than to my sisters.

It's an amazing night. As always, there is a lot of laughter, easy-going fun and interesting conversation about everything and nothing. However, I notice a shade of sadness on Ruslan's face. Obviously, he is thinking about me leaving tomorrow. Both of us try not to talk about my departure. I think we both know that there is no point in planning anything or giving each other useless vows that neither of us can keep. It is unspoken, but we both know that we'll try to keep in touch, and that if there is a chance, we will meet again.

The dinner is easy and pleasant. A bottle of vintage Chianti, some home-made pasta, a cheesecake to share for dessert, followed by a shot of grappa and a cup of hot and sweet espresso. Then Ruslan pays the bill, rejecting my offer to contribute, and insists on walking me home. As we get closer to my place we both fall silent – neither of us want this evening to end. I cheer up when Ruslan, fighting his usual sweet modesty, suggests stopping somewhere, getting a bottle of something and coming up to my place for one last drink.

It's club policy that no men are allowed in the girls' accommodation. Us girls never break those rules. But it is my last night and I don't give a shit about the rules. I smile 'yes', relieved that I don't have to say goodbye to him yet. We stop at a 24/7. Ruslan gets a small bottle of whisky, complaining that there are no good wines or champagnes available.

We make ourselves comfortable on my bed because I don't have any chairs. The room looks pretty messy with my suitcases all over the place. Instead of glasses, we use cups. It turns out to be a Soviet realism improvisation, which we keep joking about. As Ruslan pours the whisky, he accidently spills some onto the floor and his knees. I go to the kitchen to bring a cloth. When I return he is standing in the middle of the room, holding the cups and looking at me. His whole face is screaming love, tenderness and great pity at the same time.

I drop the cloth on the floor and step right in front of him. He hands me my cup without taking his eyes off me even for a second, and whispers, 'I want to drink to you, my new but precious friend, who ...' he hesitates for a second, clears his throat and continues, '... who I've fallen in love with ... with all my heart ...'

It is so moving; I'm unexpectedly emotional. We empty our cups, lean into each other, and lock in a long and passionate kiss.

The floor starts moving under my feet ... my head insanely swinging ...

27

The vigorous whack on my door wakes me, painfully echoing in my head. It is Natalia: 'Jul, the cab is downstairs! Come on, the plane is not going to wait for you, princess!'

I find myself on the floor, without any comprehension of what is going on or what my sister is talking about. I rush towards the door but unbearable dizziness forces me to sit back. I feel a sudden surge of nausea. Strange, I've never had such a bad hangover before ... and I didn't drink that much last night. I try again – slowly this time – holding onto the bed. As I move towards the door, it feels like I am on a boat riding the waves during a storm.

When I finally manage to open for Natalia, I race
to the toilet because I can't fight the retching anymore
… a couple of minutes of hugging the lavatory seat
and I feel relieved for a moment … but a second later,
I hear Natalia screaming the tonsils out of her throat.
I come out and see that all my suitcases are open and
my clothes scattered on the floor, all over the place.

'I can't believe you haven't finished packing yet!'
shouts Natalia. 'Don't you know what time the flight
is?'

I am staring at the floor, trying to understand why
the suitcases are open. I know I finished packing them
yesterday morning. I struggle to recall the events
of last night, but my head is spinning, my temples
pulsing painfully.

'Can't you act like a grown-up, just once?' continues Natalia, going down onto her knees and throwing
my stuff back into the suitcases. 'Why are you
standing like a statue, Jul, when we have five minutes
to get your ass, together with these suitcases, to the
cab?'

But I can't hear her. I am trying hard to concentrate
and understand what is going on. I drop to my knees,
too, like a zombie, repacking the clothes, tensely
doing my damnedest to recollect at least something
about last night. I notice my vanity case, which is also
lying on the floor upside down, and heavily sigh, 'No
fucking way!'

I reach for it.

Of course, the black plastic bag into which I rolled all the money I withdrew from my account a few days before – all the money I'd earned in six months – is gone.

The blood rushes into my head and another bout of nausea fills my body. Natalia storms out to the kitchen and comes back with a glass of water. Then she goes back to packing and asks, 'What the hell happened to you last night?'

I fight through the dizziness, look at her and whisper, 'The money is gone … I don't remember anything … Maybe I was spiked or something … I don't understand how that could happen.'

I sob. A stream of hot tears starts running down my cheeks.

Natalia's eyes widen as never before, but she remains quiet and doesn't stop packing my stuff. As soon as she finishes and everything is ready to be tugged down to the cab, she looks at me calmly but scornfully, and throws, 'Sure, as always …'

I stop crying, get off the floor and wipe the tears from my face. 'And what is that supposed to mean, Nata?'

Her eyes are full of disgust and disappointment.

'Haven't you noticed, Jul, how bad stuff keeps on happening to you? And that it's always somebody else's fault? Don't you find it strange? Huh? First the incident with Lena's boyfriend, then all your drug and fighting stories, and now this?'

'What? An *incident*? This is what you're calling that now? Was it my fault?'

An enormous ache hits my chest. It is unbearable, along with the pulsating kicks in my head. I think I would feel better after five rounds in the ring with both Vitali and Vladimir Klitschko at the same time.

Natalia just looks away, distant, heads to the door and hisses, 'You have five minutes to get ready. We'll be waiting in the cab.' And before she walks out of the room, she adds, 'I hope *this* you can complete without getting into trouble.'

We manage to get onto the plane in time. Neither Natalia nor I say a word all the way home. Lena tries to get us to talk and explain what happened, but soon falls silent as well.

28

I can't stop thinking about what happened. Maybe it was not Ruslan's fault at all, and he was also a victim of the robbery? I wish I could remember something. The only helpful idea that comes to me on the way home is to have a blood test as soon as I get there.

The check-up with the GP, plus the blood and urine tests, confirm that I have been poisoned.

'After two days, it is difficult to say what exactly you were poisoned with, Julia. But I can tell you that something definitely happened, and considering your symptoms, I think it was Clonidine.'

The doctor is talking to me while writing something at his desk.

Then he stops and looks at me with eyes full of concern. 'Who did you spend that night with?'

I explain what happened, insisting that Ruslan couldn't have done it to me, and that I thought there was somebody else involved.

The doctor knits his brows and continues, 'You are too naïve, young lady. He is a typical, experienced spiker. In 95 per cent of such cases, the victims think they know their beguiler very well and can trust him or her too. A Clonidine overdose is extremely dangerous, especially when consumed with alcohol. You are very lucky to be alive, Julia, and my suggestion to you would be to go to the police.'

While the doctor is giving his opinion, dizziness drowns me again and my head bursts with the pulsations in my temples. Vivid memories of Ruslan asking the 'right' questions to get the 'right' information to carry out his fucking brutal plan begin to run through my head as if I am awake but dreaming:

'For how long are you going to be working still, Jul?' 'I guess it's an exhausting job, Jul, but do you at least make good money?' His always considerate way of never impeding my working schedule – to make sure I made as much money as possible. His phone call a few days before my departure, after I'd come back from the post office with my money, extracting details of how I spent my day and what I did, covering it with his 'concern' for how tired I must be. His coming up to my room on our last date and the drink that he spilled on his pants, to make sure I wouldn't see him putting something into my glass while I went to the kitchen to get a cloth.

Everything is falling into place. It is becoming so obvious now!

Oh my fuck! It was him! That son of a bitch!

Without a doubt it was Ruslan who'd been hunting me down since the very first time we met.

Unfuckingbelievable! How stupid I was!

I go over and over our short but intense acquaintance, putting all the details together. He'd calculated everything, even the fact that I wouldn't have time to look for him or to go to the police.

I continue, recollecting the tragic life story that the motherfucker had told me with tears in his eyes, realising that even his name was most likely fake, and that I was probably not the first – or the last – idiot from which he'd stolen money. I feel like screaming in anger and desperation.

Stupid! Stupid! I am so stupid!

Most painful is to think about the last evening we spent together. How could I have been so green, so blind?

For a few days I feel nothing but rage, which shifts to a real despair that I'd lost my money and the friendship I'd enjoyed so much. This deep self-pity then mutates into a numb depression, which crumbles and chews me up from the inside. I have no idea how to escape it.

I decide not to tell my parents and ask my sisters to keep quiet about it too. Bugger all could be done to get my money back anyway – my mom and dad would get worried and upset for nothing. My sisters keep giving me looks of pity – mostly Lena, of course – and can't stop saying bullshit like, 'Everything that happens in life happens for the better', or 'Money is not everything; the most important thing is that the bastard didn't kill you,' which drives me even more nuts. That is why I go for broke to spend as little time at home as possible.

I party and consume with my pals, sleeping over at my girlfriends' places or with some random guys I hook up with in nightclubs, wasting the last of the money I have. When I was packing in Luxembourg I decided to take €1,500 out of the total I'd earned, in case I wanted to shop at the airport, and put it into my handbag. Luckily, when Ruslan had got his hands on the money in my vanity case, he'd been too generously lazy to search for more.

Oh, I hate the bastard! I hope all his limbs fall off, including his cock!

While I am busy trashing my depression and myself with booze and drugs, my sisters, after a little research and conversation with a few hooker co-workers, decide to go to France. The contract is only for three months and the waiting period can stretch up to seven weeks; what's more, the impresario fees and travel expenses make it impossible for me to go on that run.

Aside from the fact that I can't afford it, I really don't feel like going anywhere with Natalia. Since the fight in my room in Luxembourg, we've spoken only a few times, growling at each other more than speaking. Even when she found out about the doctor's explanation of what happened to me, she never came up with an apology, probably still thinking it was somehow my fault. I can't get her words out of my head and don't even try to pretend that it is 'fine' between us. It is not 'fine', and I am never going anywhere with miss-bitchy-perfection ever again.

Despite my constant comatose state, I settle on a plan of my own. During one of my nights out, I bump into Inna, one of my school friends. It turns out she is regularly contracting in Istanbul. When she hears about my situation, she suggests that I go on the next trip with her. She explains that no paperwork or waiting time is required to go there, and the 'business' is easy, describing it as a free-rider's paradise. She is planning to go back in two weeks herself.

Just a few more shots of tequila with Inna and I make up my mind.

29

In the meantime, Lena's Michel decides to come to Ukraine for a holiday. She is ecstatic – she distorts her interpretation of his visit in her usual manner, deducing that he is coming all the way here to propose to her.

Aargh ... what a hopeless dreamer ...

Natalia and I just roll our eyes and don't even try to convince her not to draw such a forward conclusion so quickly.

Michel's difficulties begin when he first starts to plan his vacation. Besides the fact that there is no functioning airport in Kherson, and that from Kiev he has to take a train, bus or taxi, turning a four to five-hour journey into a trek of 15 hours or more, the only hotel that he finds online is the three-star Soviet-era-pride inn, the Liner. When Michel sees the pictures of its rooms and 'suites' on the Internet, the scene plunges him into serious doubt. But the idea of spending some time with his Lena, and a chance to experience the country famous for its beautiful women, ancient and glorious cathedrals, and the spirit and taste of a life that was hidden by the iron curtain and soaked in communist utopianism for more than 70 years, keeps him firm about this adventure.

They both are very excited when he arrives, spending the days lollygagging and the nights partying.

Michel is getting the sought-after post-Soviet experience in full – from the local restaurants (including some trendy ones that even have menus written in English, where they serve salads drowned in mayonnaise, or chips with suspicious meat, proudly called sirloin steak, that float in a puddle of burned sunflower oil on the plate), to becoming familiar with the public toilets of 'perestroika-collapse' Ukraine.

When Michel gets off the train and waits for Lena, he realises that he very much needs to do a number two. He waits until Lena shows up, hurriedly hugs and kisses her on the cheek, asks her to watch his luggage and canters towards the sign – туалет[13] –

13 Russian, 'Toilet'

that is thoughtfully adorned with little stick figures of a man and a woman.

The toilet is a small, single-level brick block about 50 metres away from the central train station building. When Michel jumps inside, the stench hits him – a mixture of urine, crap and chlorine that burns his eyes, nostrils and throat. An old lady – the paymistress – sits in a small anteroom next to a little wooden table with a roll of greyish toilet paper and a pair of scissors in her hands. A metal plate with coins, a sign saying 50к[14], and a few pieces of evenly cut toilet paper folded next to each other decorate the table.

Michel searches his pocket, without taking his wondering eyes off the woman, grabs a handful of coins and places it on the plate. She glances at him, mutters 'спасибо'[15] and hands him one of the toilet paper pieces. Michel slowly takes the sheet, staring at it, and starts shaking his head, knowing that it wouldn't be enough for his morning evacuation. He thinks for a second, impatiently shifting from one foot to another, and then takes a €10 bill from another pocket. He waves the bill right in front of the old lady's face while pointing at the roll in her hand. The woman smiles, takes the money and hands him the whole roll.

---

14 Russian, short for 'cents'

15 Russian, 'Thanks'

Michel, satisfied with himself, walks into the loo holding the toilet paper as if it's some kind of trophy. The scenery inside makes him stop in a complete shock. There are no toilet seats – instead, there are only four tiled holes in the floor, separated by brick walls with no doors to give people any privacy. The floor around the holes is smeared with dirt, crap and urine; huge green flies hum around and enliven the picture.

Ha ha! Poor Michel! His spoilt European eyes never saw anything like that before!

The rest of his vacation goes quite pleasantly until the day before his departure.

He and Lena are walking back to his hotel after having a romantic dinner in one of the restaurants. At the hotel's entrance they stop to have a cigarette. They're busy discussing something, and don't notice the teenager who walks out of the darkness and heads towards them. The young man asks for a cigarette, and when Lena pulls one out of the box, he thanks her and leaves.

A few minutes later, the same guy comes back, with another five yobbos of the same age, holding cudgels. They approach the couple too quickly for Lena and Michel to realise that they are in trouble. They punch Michel without any warning, throwing him onto the pavement and kicking him with their boots. Then one of them starts searching Michel's

pockets and pulls out his wallet and passport. Lena
begs them not to take his passport and credit cards,
hysterically explaining that they would not be able to
use them anyway. The one who asked for a cigarette,
probably the 'big brother', pulls a knife, points it
at her and threatens, 'Shut up bitch! Let's see what
you've got in your purse?' They take all their cash,
their watches and my sister's gold earrings, but they
listen to what Lena said and throw the passport and
the cards back onto the ground. The one with the
knife directs again, 'Come on guys, let's get out of
here.' Before they disappear, he scornfully utters,
'Don't cry, baby, your fuck will not grow poor; in the
meantime, we also need to eat.'

Lena helps Michel off the ground and they both
hobble to the hotel's lobby, where she calls a cab and
they go to the nearest hospital. The doctor in the
emergency room checks Michel and X-rays the parts
of his body that hurt the most. Turns out that he has
a small crack in his rib, minor bruises all over his
body, and broken glasses. He also twisted his wrist
when they knocked him down onto the pavement.

The doctor gives Michel some painkillers, a sling
for his arm and a written report for the police. Lena
calls another cab and they go to the police station.

It is late, and the station is empty and quiet. When
the officer on duty shows up, he looks at the couple as
if they've disturbed his slumber. He tries to put some
interest and concern onto his face while Lena tells

their story, but he still can't hide his testiness. When she finishes, he smirks, narrows his eyes and looks at my sister.

'What is your working nickname, miss?' he asks knowingly, staring at her.

Lena, thrown off balance, lifts her eyebrows. 'Excuse me?'

'Well, miss, what I see here is a slightly different version of the story you have just told me. It's obvious to me that you are just some local prostitute, who works that area to hook up with the hotel guests. First, you wormed yourself into the confidence of this Mr Rich Foreigner, then you gave him away to the gang of young yobbos you work with. Am I right, miss?' He pauses condescendingly, looking very satisfied with his deduction skills, and continues.

'Would you still like to proceed with your statement and with letting us investigate this robbery? Or maybe you should go back to the hotel and fuck your client as you are supposed to, and stop wasting my time and the taxpayers' money?'

Freaking Hercule Poirot!

The words shove Lena into shock and she can't find words to answer him. Her face goes pale and her eyes fill with tears. 'Lena, sweetheart, what is he saying? Why are you upset?' Michel is so confused.

She looks at him and whispers, 'I think we are done here, Michel. Let's go back to the hotel …'

Totally mixed up, he gets up off his chair and mutters, 'Of course … let's go. Are you sure you don't want to tell me what he said to you?'

Lena shakes her head and they leave.

The next day, Michel leaves. Lena decides to accompany him all the way to Kiev, to Borispol International. Michel's cracked rib and injured arm make it really difficult for him to manage his luggage. Also, Lena still believes that he's keeping his surprise proposal until the last moment, that right there in the airport he will go down on one knee, pull a little red velvet box from nowhere and make her the happiest woman in the world …

Seriously … what's wrong with this woman?

Michel does get onto one knee when they arrive at the airport, but only to tie his shoelace. And the only vow he gives her is to call her when he gets home. When she comprehends that there will be no proposal, the tears blur her eyes.

'Oh, don't cry, baby. I will see you soon. Right?'

She nods her head, grateful for his not-so-piercing nature.

Another heartbreaking drama for Lena, which I very much doubt teaches her anything – again. She cries all the way back to Kherson. She has nothing left but to find a justification for why he didn't propose to her ('He is not ready yet', or 'He is just too scared of his strong feelings for me').

She pulls herself together and concentrates on the trip to France.

30

Having lost the opportunity to buy the flat in Kiev, Natalia decisively jumps into research about how else she and Lena can lay out their money. This is one thing I guess I've always admired about my big sister – even though she is still angry with me for ruining that perfect investment opportunity that we could pull off only if all three of us threw money in, she never wasted a minute of her time on blame or regret, looking straight away for ways to solve the problem.

Since our return from Luxembourg, she's been checking the local newspapers every day and spending hours at the Internet café digging for any tips or clues about what would work best for the amount of money she and Lena had.

A few days ago she overheard two old gossiping neighbours talking about one of their mutual friends, who was moving to Moscow to live with her boyfriend and was selling her business ...

'Can you believe it? Our bourgeoise madam peroxided her hair to a noxious white. She thinks it makes her look twenty again,' one of the neighbours enthusiastically dished the dirt to the other.

'But have you seen the boyfriend? At least ten years younger than her. He's obviously after her money ...' splashed out of the other neighbour's mouth.

Natalia politely butted into the conversation, interrogated the grannies, and a few minutes later was on her way to the business a few blocks away from our home.

It was a two-bedroom apartment on the first floor of a typical nine-storey apartment building (identical to the one that my family and all other post-Soviet-zone folk lived in), which had been turned into a not-so-fancy but clean and successful hair salon.

A metal staircase ran from the ground to a gap in the balcony wall, which was the main entrance. The balcony itself had been transformed into a little waiting area, which led to a room that was the men's section. From there, a modestly sized passage led to the second room. It was considerably bigger than the first, fully equipped with washbasins, hooded hair dryers and big mirrors, and was reserved for the female clientele.

Natalia loved the scene and contacted the owner right away. Her name was Sophie. She was a very pleasant and intelligent woman (although the grannies were right – it did look like she overused the peroxide) and made Natalia feel like they had been good friends forever. Their conversation stayed warm and friendly, even while they negotiated the price.

An hour later, my sister had a deal she was happy with: the price was affordable and included the business, all the equipment, and the flat itself. Sophie then asked Natalia to stay for another cup of coffee and discuss a few more things about the salon's current staff members.

'You know, Natalia, I feel that I am kind of responsible for those people. And I will not sell my business if I am not sure I've protected them … they all are good people with fairly good skills …'

Natalia found this quite reasonable and agreed to sign a three-month employment contract for the staff. 'And then, obviously, it will all depend on their professionalism and discipline,' my sister reasoned, and they shook hands on the deal.

In any case, there was no salary involved as the staff worked on 30 per cent commission. It was a fair number, considering that the products, like shampoos and hair colours, were the salon's responsibility. That way, Natalia and Lena could be sure that their stylists used quality products and were as motivated and interested in the success of the business as they were.

Natalia was very excited and kept sharing her dreams with Lena about how they would run their new business. When I caught one of their tête-à-têtes in the kitchen I couldn't stop myself. *My inner green monster was out of control.*

'Great idea, Nata! Your hairdressers are honestly going to give you your 70 per cent while you're in France? Yeah, right! You are going to become businesswoman of the year.'

Natalia just shushed me, 'No one was talking to you, Jul.' And they went back to their discussion.

Nevertheless, she took my words into consideration and called our mother in Istanbul, asking her to come back and help them with the new business.

At first Mom protested, explaining that she knew nothing about hair and was scared that she wouldn't be able to pull it off. But Natalia reassured her, explaining that the business needed a manager who would keep an eye on the staff and deal with the everyday admin work.

'Besides, it's been too long for you and dad to be living apart. You know it can't last this way. This is a great opportunity for you to reunite,' my sister added, and Mother didn't resist for much longer. She did feel very lonely away from her family. So she agreed.

31

I'm finishing packing my bags as Natalia walks in to the room.

'Rethink this, Jul. I lived in Turkey for five years. It's not as good as your friend promises it is. Let's go to France together. I will lend you the money. Lena and I will help you.' Her voice is filled with genuine concern.

'I don't need your help! Leave me alone. I don't want to add more troubles in your life, as you're always saying I do.' I continue throwing my clothes into the open suitcase on the floor. *This adds quite a dramatic effect to my words.*

Natalia sighs and sits down on the bed.

'Don't be like that, Jul. I care. We all care about you ... and you know that.'

I try to avoid eye contact with her – I know she has expressions in her stash of manipulative tools that can be very convincing, 'Nata, just leave me alone. I don't have much time. I am telling you, I am going to Turkey and it's not open for discussion ... especially not with you.'

She jumps off the bed, swinging instantly from I-am-your-best-friend-in-the-world to bitchy-furious. 'Okay! You think you are clever? Fine, but just don't run back here when you get into trouble. Again.'

The fact that I can make her lose it, even for a minute, makes me feel so good. I just calmly smile back at her: 'Are you done?'

'Julia, your cab is here.' Father's shout from the kitchen interrupts our clash. 'Hurry up! Where is your luggage? I will help you to bring it down.'

I drag my suitcases and walk past Natalia without saying a word.

32

'To the river port, please,' I instruct the cab driver, and light a cigarette.

When I first hear about the transport Inna has chosen, I'm shocked. Almost two days on a small cargo ship that doesn't take more than 36 passengers and that is going to sail through the waves – and possibly storms – of the Black Sea, doesn't sound like a cracking plan at all. But after giving it a lot of thought I get that it's not as bad an idea as it first looked. My suitcases can be as heavy as I need them to be, and I can take more than one, without paying anything extra. A one-way ticket is $80, twice or even three times cheaper than an air ticket. Even though our travel time will be much longer than if we flew, we still have cabins in which to sleep flat, and dining three times a day. And because it is summer, we can suntan on beach chairs on the deck. What's more, it's something I've never done before. I wouldn't call it excitement, but I do have some kind of curiosity about what it feels like to be on the open sea.

By the time I drag my two suitcases out of the cab and straight into the port's only shabby bar, which is packed with passengers and oversized checked polypropylene bags that are a signature item of the shuttle traders all over the post-Soviet space, my former schoolmate is already pretty hammered. She sticks persistently to the good-looking barman with confidence on her drunken phiz and refuses to notice his I-am-not-interested-in-you-soaker-why-don't-you-just-shut-up expression.

When she sees me, she starts an uncoordinated waving while holding on to the bar. Her body language screams that if it wasn't for the old, dark-wood counter, she would be on the floor already.

'Oh my ... Inna! You are loaded, my friend. It's a good thing we have to board in a few minutes, so you can get some sleep.' I talk softly, as if she is a five-year-old.

She rolls her eyes and throws a discharge of loud laughter into the air. 'Did you just say minutes? Not so fast, my friend! These bastards are going to marinate us overnight like some fucking chicken drumsticks!'

She bursts into more laughter. Then suddenly her face darkens, her body sways and she starts to fall off the bar stool.

'Here we are!' I catch Inna under the arms. Her eyes mist in drowsiness and her head drops heavily to the side. I help her to relocate to one of the soft chairs that a young man is using; he courteously vacates it for us. Without coming back to the world, she sprawls in a not-so-elegant position with her legs spread wide, passed out. I bring a glass of water and put it on the table next to her. Then I go back to the bar, notice the disgust on the barman's face, mumble to myself, 'I must put "get drunk as a pig" on my not-to-do list … it's really ugly,' and order a double vodka with orange juice.

I sip my drink, look at my watch and scowl – we were supposed to board at least twenty minutes ago. The barman notes the concern on my face and snoops, 'Is it your first time?'

I raise my eyebrows and look at him, searching for some kind of sarcasm or a taunt, but am surprised to see a friendly smile on his attractive face.

Oh dear! He looks like a normal guy. I wonder how much Inna tormented and annoyed him to put him in the twitching state he was in half an hour ago?

I smile and nod.

'Don't expect to board anytime soon. Sometimes it takes the whole day and night. They are still busy loading the cargo. And until they finish, they will keep you guys waiting here,' he explains with ease.

My eyes widen, and 'Fuck!' flies out of my mouth before I even think about it.

The barman smiles at that and goes to serve another client.

Seven hours, three screwdrivers, four cups of coffee and a full pack of cigarettes later, at three o'clock in the morning, one of the crew comes up and announces that all passengers can proceed to the passport control section.

Half asleep, irritated folk begin to rumble, get off their seats and pull their trunks out onto the street. I wake Inna and we follow the crowd. We quickly pass through passport control and customs. And as soon as we step on board the Victoria, we receive keys to our cabin. One of the sailors helps us to get our luggage up through a few companionways, dropping it at a door numbered 8, which is the number on our key's tag.

The cabin is a small room with a tiny cupboard and washbasin on the left, a bunk bed on the right, and a little table with one chair between them, right under the porthole. We are so wiped out that the moment we walk inside, Inna wearily drops, 'I am sleeping at the bottom ... I get seasick,' and crawls, still dressed, under the blanket. I murmur, 'No wonder ... drinking so much,' and climb onto the top bunk, without even brushing my teeth or washing my make-up off. Two minutes later we zonk out into a deep sleep.

The next day I wake up and for a few seconds I can't work out where I am. I close my eyes again and drown in thoughts about my life and where it is taking me this time. A light rush of adrenalin shivers through my body when I think of what kind of crap I could get myself into on this trip. No place to stay, no friends or people in whom I can have at least an illusion of trust and reliance, no working contract, no working permit.

In other words, a total fuck-up if something goes wrong.

I spend most of the trip on my own. Part of me is grateful that Inna has such an urge to get wasted and fuck some sailors, whose names I bet she can't even remember the next day. Her drunken brawls give me some quiet time to myself. I try to catch up on some sleeping and tan on the deck with a book and a chilled beer.

When we approach the Bosphorus Strait it is night-time. At first it is impossible to distinguish the shoreline, because of how it merges with the dark sea and sky. Then, some lights start to appear, showing us the coast on both sides of the ship. The deeper we get into the strait, the more alive the land looks. When finally we reach Istanbul, I can't believe my eyes. It is the most beautiful thing I've ever seen! The view is breathtaking …

We ride the waves between the two headlands that rise uphill, covered by millions and millions of lights. We pass under the two huge bridges that connect the Asian and European parts of the metropolis and remind me of a graceful Christmas-light garland. The city glows. The mosques, whose minarets are adorned with floodlights of different colours, add to the city's mood. Istanbul is alive and captivating; immense and powerful. It treacherously expands the space inside me for disturbing thoughts, bringing forth my fears and relentlessly emphasizing my vulnerability.

After making our way through the Bosphorus for about two hours, the Victoria berths at Istanbul's Karaköy Port. I am still standing on deck, gazing around, absorbed, as my thoughts about my slippery tomorrow deepen.

The loud voice of the same person who announced the boarding in Kherson pulls me out of myself and into reality. He is walking around, warning passengers – with a smirk – to get ready for passport control. 'Dear friends! Please go to your cabins and pack your stuff. The Turkish authorities will be on board in an hour or so. And ladies, I know it has been a long and tiring journey for some of you ...' He stops his eyes on Inna for a second, filled with satisfied lust – *Oh gosh, she slept with him too! Although 'sleeping' is probably not the right word for what they were doing ...* – then continues, 'Please make sure you remember your surnames, the ones that are in your passports!'

I look at Inna with genuine surprise. 'What does he mean?'

She rolls her eyes.

Her day-after sickness has severe symptoms. No wonder – she hasn't been sober for over two days. She talks quietly and slowly, as if the words are stinging her. 'Many girls have been deported for illegal prostitution or working without a permit. To come back, they arrange sham marriages and get new passports with their new surnames. The problem is that these bitches get so wasted during the trip ...' Inna's tone is surprisingly judgmental – *she obviously doesn't consider herself to be one of them!* – '... and often can't remember their new surnames when the authorities call them out for their turn. It usually turns ugly: they are deported again without even getting off the ship, and it delays the other passengers as well.'

She looks at me and frowns, most likely because of her headache. 'Let's go and pack, Jul. We don't have much time.'

33

The morning after we arrive, Inna receives a phone call from one of her clients. Because we sleep in one bed in the small and scruffy studio she rents on a regular basis, the ringing wakes us both up.

I open my eyes and close them again. I am worn out. I barely slept last night. Passport control and customs went quickly and smoothly, but we still only got to Inna's place at 2 a.m. and were in bed by about 3 a.m.

I was so tired when we left the port that I struggled to keep my eyes open in the taxi, but the moment my head hit the pillow my anxious thoughts started to crawl back, wiping my sleepiness away completely.

At about 5 a.m. I finally fell asleep, but was kicked awake right away by a man's very weird singing over loudspeakers somewhere close by, out on the street. I jumped out of bed, thinking it was a bomb or fire alarm, but then spotted, through our window, the mosque: its two minarets had freaking speakers on them. I remembered Natalia telling me about it. It was Namaz, the call to prayer, performed five times a day through the squawk boxes of every mosque.

As soon as Inna finishes her short conversation on the phone she energetically jumps out of bed.

'Time to get up, Jul. I've got some work for us this afternoon, but we still have to do shopping and get ready for it.'

I frown and moan theatrically. I am tired and don't want to get up.

She sticks her head out of the bathroom. With the toothbrush in her mouth and white foam on her lips, she mumbles, 'Come on, princess! Time to make some money. The guy is a freak but at least he pays well.'

We do a quick shop for some toiletries and food, then stop at the pharmacy, where we buy some regular tampons, Pharmatex sponges[16], some laxative pills – two of which Inna takes straight away – and a lot of ultra thin condoms. As my new roommate casually

---

16 A contraceptive sponge that women often use during menstruation to stop the bleeding during intercourse.

explains, Turkish men hate to use a rubber, so this is her compromise. Then we go back home, eat some brunch and start getting ready for work.

'Taxim please,' orders Inna, when we climb into the cab.

I light a cigarette and take a deep and comforting drag. 'This morning you said this guy is a freak. Are you planning on telling me anything about what we're gonna have to do?' I do not even try to hide the irritation in my voice.

Inna lights a cigarette herself and coolly explains, 'What you will have to do is hold the camera. The freak likes to film his sessions. I will do the rest. Easy money, Jul, isn't it?'

I sigh with relief. I hope it's as she says. Then it will be easy money for real and I can relax and stop worrying.

When we walk into the hotel lobby, Inna confidently heads to the front desk. 'Mr Emir is waiting for us in room number ...' she hesitates, looks again at her text messages, '... room number ... 539.'

The receptionist is a young man. He gives us a look that screams, 'I know you are whores. If it were up to me I would have you thrown out of this place!' but picks up the phone and dials to contact the room. After a quick pause, he puts a submissive look back on his face and murmurs, 'Mr Emir, you have visitors.' Then he nods, puts the receiver down and waves to us that we can go.

'Wow, what was that all about?' I ask Inna, who is already in the elevator.

'Bloody morons! You see, the problem is that there are too many of us handy Eastern European women, well-known for our beauty, screwing all over Istanbul and making money. These men are Muslim. Most of them hate us because of their inner conflict.' Inna pauses, searching for the right words. 'To them, we are depraved. They have to feel pure aversion for us, and they do – until they see us. But because we are so gorgeous and sexy,' she smirks, giving herself an approving look in the elevator's mirror, 'as soon as they *do* see us, their aversion fades and all they can think about is how great it would be if they could climb on top of us themselves. In other words, we make them want to betray their religion, their beliefs, and their usually fat and useless-in-bed wives.'

'Wow! Interesting theory,' I praise Inna as we walk out of the elevator.

She is not stupid, but all that alcohol she consumes doesn't complement her intellect at all.

Some time after we knock, the door opens on a barefoot man pressing a folded white terry robe with a missing belt to his waist. He is not a bad-looking guy. He smiles, hugs Inna, and starts chattering something like 'Come on in' and 'Glad to see you again'.

Turns out it is not a room but a suite. It's spacious, beautifully furnished, with a reception area; the bedroom is separated by a TV stand. He offers us a drink. Before leaving to the bar, he hands Inna the money. 'You know what I want you to do, right?'

She thanks him and drags me to the bathroom. As soon as the door closes behind us, she quickly counts the money in front of me. There are eight hundred-dollar bills; she puts five into her bag and gives three to me. Then she starts peeling her clothes off while giving me instructions. 'He likes to be nude. All the time we spend here we also have to be naked. So hurry up and let's go have a drink. I need a boost before we start,' she frowns. Absolutely naked, she leaves the bathroom.

When I walk out, both of them are standing *au naturel* in the middle of the room and nonchalantly discussing the weather or some other bullshit that is a far cry from our current situation.

My eyes whip through the man's figure: middle-aged, not too tall, not fat, but with a little beer-stomach, and not athletically built either. Then I stop my gaze at Inna. Her body is flawless. She is quite thin but with a nice ass and beautiful tits that make her look less bony and much sexier than me.

I join them and receive a glass of chilled champagne, which we clink and toast, '*Şerefe!*'[17]

I take a sip, while Inna drains the whole glass at once and hurriedly asks for another one. The man

_____

17 Turkish, 'Cheers'

refills it and with a nervous smirk invites us to the bedroom.

He gives me a little camera and explains how to use it.

I hadn't noticed when we came in, but see now that a big vinyl mat covers most of the bed. I switch the camera on and give a thumbs-up, indicating that I am ready to record.

He lies down on his back. His legs hang down without touching the floor. He closes his eyes and takes a deep breath: 'I am ready too.'

Inna stands on the bed with her legs spread so he is caught between them. The moment she does this, I know what is about to happen. I smile to myself, recalling my own experience of peeing in the client's mouth while Natalia worked him, down on her knees.

But the chain of my thoughts is interrupted. What I'm seeing now makes me want to vomit. I cover my mouth with one hand while trying to hold the camera still with the other.

No fucking way!

Inna squats, her pussy right in front of his chin. He stares at it as if his whole life depends on it and slowly touches his organ. After a short moment, the crap starts running out of Inna's ass right onto his chest. It is not even normal, 'healthy' ca-ca, but a loose and extremely smelly one.

The two laxative pills Inna took that morning make sense to me now.

While she relieves herself, producing some generous farts at the same time, he uses one hand to smear her stream all over his body, including his face and mouth, which he doesn't even try to keep shut. With his other hand, he masturbates his pulsing, erect tool.

Oh my fuck! He is actually hard! What's wrong with this man?

When Inna is done, she slowly stands up and carefully gets off the bed, leaving him alone in the mud of her crap. She walks out of the room and comes back in a second with some wet wipes and another full glass of champagne.

Unbelievable! What's wrong with this woman?!

If I've understood everything correctly, her part of the job is done, but I still have to film the creepy movie.

He spreads Inna's poop evenly over his body ...

Oh, by the way, good job covering the bed with plastic.

Then, without standing up, he turns around so that his legs point towards the headboard. He slithers using his elbows until his flexed knees are touching the panel. Then he lifts his legs up into a fucking sarvangasana[18], using his hands to support his lower back.

My right hand is tired; I shift the camera into my left hand without taking my eyes off the scene even

---

18 Yoga position also known as the Shoulder Stand

for a second. The sickest, weirdest, weirdo-yogi ever is so flexible that when he lowers his hips to his head, his penis reaches his mouth. The rest takes him a few minutes – he sucks his own dick and ejaculates into his mouth.

Unfuckingbelievable! What on earth made him even come up with the idea of blowing himself?

Fifteen minutes later we are in a cab on the way home. We both light a cigarette and stay quiet for some time. I can't believe that what I saw happened for real. I try to think positively and delete the images from my head. I switch to the $300 that I made in one hour just by being naked and holding a camera. I even start to think that I could get used to the creepy man and do it all again. Inna breaks the silence and pulls me out of my thoughts.

'Yeah, he is totally fucked up, but he's also the only one who pays this kind of money, Julia, so don't shoot for the sky.'

I remain quiet and just sigh; in that one moment she's made me forget about the yogi and dragged me back to my troubled thoughts about this trip. Just a week ago she was telling me what a moneymaking paradise this is, and now she's saying 'don't shoot for the sky' …

Aargh! I know this run is going to be a fuck-up … Please, please, please let Natalia be wrong … at least this once …

'Jul, what do you say we stop at Migros[19] to get some beers? I have a few Russian movies we could watch.' I nod 'Sure.' Inna continues, 'Trust me, there is no way we are going to be able to eat anything today anyway.'

I close my eyes and my body shudders with disgust.

---

19 One of the supermarket chains in Turkey.

34

For the first time in a few weeks I actually have a good night's sleep; even the 5 a.m. call to prayer doesn't wake me up. We get up at about ten, make some coffee, and both engage in finishing unpacking and organising all our stuff so it can fit into the small apartment.

Then we eat a quick lunch and head to a meeting with Inna's present and my future employer – our pimp.

'I have a few direct clients,' Inna explains as we walk through the many narrow, busy streets, mostly paved with stones, towards the ferry station. Our whoremaster resides on the Asian side of the city, so we have to cross the Bosphorus Strait to see her.

'I mean, I work for these clients without Alexandra's mediation, like yesterday's one. Please make sure you don't mention this to her.'

I nod, taking a deep breath. The streets are filled with the smells of fried fish and freshly baked foods, wrapped up in the strong scent of the sea.

'She is a normal mama, also from Ukraine, but I do hate her deep inside of me.' Inna keeps a good pace; her words start to come out broken as her breathing gets puffy. 'I hate her especially when she gets me some fucker who cannot come for hours …' She pauses to look for cars before crossing the street. 'I get fucked until my poor pussy falls off and then I have to share my hard-earned money with her.' Inna interrupts her discourse as we stop to buy tokens for the ferry. We go through the turnstile and Inna heads straight for the deck. 'Let's sit outside so we can smoke.' We settle on the right side of the ship, on a long bench that curves through the full length of the boat.

'So yes,' continues Inna, lighting a cigarette and passing me the lighter, 'my cracked-up vagina versus a few damn phone calls does not sound fair to me at all, especially when she takes 50 per cent.'

I keep nodding while staring at the view. It is incredibly beautiful: the Bosphorus glowing in the sun, the blue sky with soaring seagulls, the shore, moving away now, tightly stuffed with thousands of featureless buildings, and the mirrored skyscrapers, mosques, and ancient palaces and towers scattered here and there between them. The breathtaking view has such a strong effect on me …

'Of course, I understand that somebody has to do her job,' Inna starts again, 'and I know she finds us more clients so we can make more money, but I cannot help it, Jul, and still hate the bitch.' We both giggle and light another cigarette.

Alexandra is about 30 years old, a good-looking blonde with a petite body like mine. It's obvious that this woman looks after herself. Her smile shows me a mouth full of perfect teeth as she checks me out from head to toe as if I were a sale item somewhere on the free market.

'The demands are simple. You always have to be at your phone, and you need to learn to get ready as quickly as possible.' *I assume that her starting to explain the rules of the business means that I am a suitable item with a good chance of getting sold.* 'Most of the time, the client calls one or two hours before he would like his order to be delivered. Considering Istanbul's traffic, there is usually very little time for long showers and complicated make-up. Although I hope I don't need to mention that you always have to look your best.'

The waitress comes around and all three of us order coffee.

'We're going to work a 50/50 split for the first three months, and then, if you are good, I may consider a 70/30 split, as I'm doing with Inna now.' They grin at each other and I just do my nodding.

'Because of the overloaded market, we have to keep our prices reasonable. One hour is $100. If he wants you for the night, then it's $150. Tips and taxi fares are not obligatory for the clients, but you are welcome to ask for them, and most of the time they give some without a problem.'

An unvarying smile is glued to her face, somehow transforming it from pretty to seriously annoying.

This phoniness of hers is screaming at me: 'Jul! This Istanbul run is going to be a fuck-up!' Why can't I just listen, pack my stuff and get the fuck out of here?

'I guess this is it, Julia. Would you like to use your real name or change it?'

I shrug my shoulders and give Inna my what-should-I-do? look. She playfully shrugs her shoulders back to me, indicating that she can't help me on this one and that I'll have to decide for myself. I take a sip of my already cold coffee.

'I want to change it to Victoria.'

Alexandra takes her time to check something in her black leather notepad, then agrees while putting on the same fake expression again. 'No problem, I don't have anybody else with this name.'

We exchange numbers and she stands up to go.

'Don't worry. You are going to be fine. All Turkish men love skinny blonde girls, so I guarantee you a busy working schedule. Trust me, Victoria.' She winks at me, kisses the air twice – once at me and once at Inna – and hurriedly leaves.

'Why can't we work for ourselves?' I ask Inna, with a hint of despair after Alexandra disappears behind the door, knowing the answer to my question already.

'We could, Jul, but where would we find clients?'

I should probably have kept quiet and not have rubbed it in, because she sounds very irritated: 'One of the options is to go to a few nightclubs in Laleli or Aksaray. These are places where working girls and clients look for each other. The only problem is that this can be extremely dangerous: your clients are strangers who take you to their own places. No guarantees that one of them is not a maniac or some psychopath. What's more, the police raid those areas regularly. If you are caught, you go home, leaving all your belongings and money here, with a red "Deported" stamp in your passport.'

'And you called it a free-rider's paradise … no shit!' I pull a grave face and wave to the waitress for the bill.

35

As Inna and I enter our apartment, my phone starts ringing.

'Hi Victoria. It's Alexandra. Didn't expect me to call you so soon?' Her voice is much softer on the phone. I guess it is her professional strategy – to sound sexy and welcoming to her clients.

'I have some work for you this evening. It's only for one hour, but if the client likes you he might keep you for the night. It's in Beşiktaş. Start getting ready. I will send you all the details via SMS.' She hangs up.

I slowly put my cellphone on the kitchen counter, mumble to Inna, who is looking curiously at me, 'It was our mama – I have a job to do tonight,' and turn towards the bathroom.

Inna is surprised.

'Really? She must have liked you a lot, Jul.' She shouts so I can hear her through the water splashing in the shower.

I peel my clothes off and step under the hot stream. The phone call made me so nervous that my hands are shaking and my heart is racing. Why do I feel this way? I went through a lot in Luxembourg, but have never felt this panicky before. I guess hooking up with a potential client in a cabaret, having a few words with him, and having a chance to make my own judgement of him before agreeing to go out with him is completely different from having to walk into some hotel room or apartment and put my safety into the hands of a complete stranger I have never seen or even spoken to before.

Yes, of course I could have made an error of judgement back then too, and got myself into trouble, but for the whole six months that I worked there I hadn't been raped or drugged – except for that naphthalene bastard, (with whom, by the way, it was not my instinct that failed, it screamed at me not to go, but my greed that treacherously exposed me) and Ruslan, but that is a different story that could have happened to anyone. I shiver and put my face into the hot water, trying to wash the unpleasant memories out of my mind.

On the other hand, the fact that I work through Alexandra may guarantee my protection – although in a very flimsy way. Most of her clients are people she knows, or the friends of those people, or the friends of those friends … which means that our mama has some useful contacts for finding a girl if she gets into trouble. So there is some sort of security. Unless, of course, the client happens to lose his mind and stops worrying about the consequences of his aggression … or Alexandra's rescue action is too slow; or … *Crap, what am I thinking!*

I leave the bathroom full of steam, wrapped in a towel and my not-very-optimistic thoughts. I carefully browse through my wardrobe looking for the right dress to wear: sexy enough to make me look desirable, but not too revealing, so I don't feel uneasy. Then I grab my vanity case, sit on the bed and start doing my make-up. The phone buzzes, texting me the address, time, cellphone number and name of my rendezvous. I look at my watch, trying to ignore my anxious heartbeat, thinking about how a shot or two of tequila or a little joint would definitely calm me down.

'Do you want me to call you a cab?' Inna asks, removing her headset. She is sitting on her side of the bed and watching a movie on her computer. I nod, without taking my eyes off the little mirror, applying another coat of mascara to my already heavily made up eyelashes.

I finish my make-up, put on the black dress I've chosen (not too short, but still quite sexy) and my summer high heels that are graced with multi-coloured stones, and stuff my little black purse with condoms, cigarettes, money for the cab, and a few tampons, *just in case*. I almost forget the photocopy of my passport (the front page and the page with the visa) that we made earlier today on the way home. As Inna explained with an I-am-so-smart expression on her face as she handed my passport to the guy in the copy shop, 'Trust me, Jul, you really do not want to lose your passport, but you still have to carry ID. So this is my compromise number two.'

I frown, remembering her compromise number one – the ultra thin condoms – kiss her on the cheek, say 'Wish me luck!' and head outside, where the taxi is already waiting for me.

36

The cab pulls up at the apartment building. According to the driver, who looks very suspicious *(I guess all of them, with their dark hair, and even darker eyes, a couple of days' bristle on their faces, finished with a set and severe stare, look suspicious to me)*, it's the right place. I dial the number that Alexandra sent me earlier.

'Hello ... Murat? It's Ju– it's Victoria. I am here.' I exhale.

The man on the other end of the line okays and tells me that he is coming down to let me in.

I ask the cab driver to wait until my 'date' shows up. Two minutes later, a man steps out of the entrance and waves towards the car. As I climb out of the back seat, making sure that my skirt is in the right place, Murat approaches the car, asks the driver how much I owe him, and pays.

Hmmm … that is a pleasant start to the evening …

We walk up the stairs to the third floor and enter the apartment. Only after the door is closed, Murat smiles, extends his hand to me and with a heavy accent (*at least he speaks English*), introduces himself: 'Nice to meet you … come on in … Victoria, right?'

He is a tall, young chap with friendly eyes and a charming smile. I shake his hand, also smile and follow him along a short passage into a spacious living room. It's fitted out with big, heavy couches and a huge fretted coffee table; two cabinets stuffed with a display of plates, glasses, and white and blue crockery stand between big potted plants. The interior looks rich, but it's old-fashioned, and doesn't match Murat's youth and his trendy clothes.

I bet it's his parents' place. They are probably away, so he can finally enjoy his temporary manhood and independence. In his late twenties and still living with his parents? Loser!

The coffee table catches my attention: glass of whisky on the rocks, ashtray full of cigarette butts, large dark ceramic plate, used as a tray, with two tidy white-powder lines and a tiny but very promising white mountain.

Murat shows me to the couch, and notices my stare. 'I hope you don't mind …' he says.

Then, 'Would you like to have a drink, Victoria?' he asks, with care. 'Yes please – the same as you,' I answer and my eyes lock, again, onto the big plate.

I cannot help it! That's exactly what my tortured nerves need tonight …

Within a few minutes we are settled on the couch, holding our frosted whisky glasses. A few gulps later, I am pressed into the backrest, Murat's possessive hand searching under my skirt while his confused jelly tongue wanders inside my mouth.

Urgh! I guess if he could kiss properly, there would be some devoted girlfriend next to him instead of me right now …

To endure these moments of sharp displeasure or disgust, I've learned to disconnect my brain from my body. I imagine, for example, that my mouth is not a part of my body any more. It helps me to fight the natural urge to tense my muscles and the impulse to push the sponger away from me.

Luckily the 'kiss' doesn't last long and Murat finally proposes, in a sweet and courteous manner, that I take a hit. I do not hesitate and drown myself in the feeling that starts off pleasantly numb then grows into a stream of energy and sexual arousal.

He pulls me off the couch and drags me into the bedroom. There, he throws me onto the bed, and tears off our clothes, giving me just a second to roll the rubber onto his erection. He lets me do it but I notice the displeasure on his face. It reminds me again about Inna's compromise number one.

The kid crawls on top of me, resting his forehead on the pillow, and starts banging me – thrusting and digging my slit, *allegretto furioso*[20], as deep as he can go. I have no choice but to stare at the white ceiling.

I don't know how much time has passed, but my pussy is completely dry now and starts to hurt. The euphoria from the coke has vanished, shifting to an annoying drowsiness and irritation. I wait and wait, dreaming of him coming and us snorting some more. But no – no such luck.

'Let me fuck you without rubber! I am clean, you can trust me!' Murat's passionate jabber draws me away from the chandelier. 'I am sorry, it's not that I don't trust you, but I don't fuck without condoms,' I answer, trying to sound congenial but with firmness in my voice.

He moans in frustration, lifts me up, turns me onto all fours, and, even more vigorously, begins to fuck me from behind. Some indefinite time later, which feels like forever, I realise what the phrase 'to fuck the shit out of someone' means.

---

20 Italian, music term: *allegretto*, meaning a moderately fast tempo; *furioso*, meaning an angry and furious way of playing.

Eventually he gets tired, and flabbily falls on top of my back. Wetting me all over with his sweat, he presses me flat into the mattress.

'*Aşkım!*[21]' he starts again, rolling the worn-out condom off his still-hard dick. 'I beg you, let me come,' he continues, fidgeting his erection against my ass.

'I am sorry, I can't,' I say, pumping even more strictness into my voice.

He sighs and stays silent for some time, and then starts again … he says the same words over and over, ignoring my rejection, topping up his speech with new, stupid arguments.

'I will have you for the night and tip you well … we'll have some more fun with the nose candy … please, Victoria … I am not sick …' He goes on and on, pretending not to hear my response.

Then, Murat starts slowly pushing his dick between my legs. After his annoying, non-stop efforts, I'm too tired to resist. I want it to be over, and 'his way' definitely seems to be the easiest. Yet I hold my muscles tight, showing my resolution. I know he is not going to force me. He is just waiting for me to give up. It is up to me to decide and I am definitely not going to change my mind …

Arghhh!

---

21 Turkish, 'My love!'

But if I resist, he will be displeased, and I will have to get up, dress and go home with no tip or money for the cab. I will be stressed, instead of having fun with my white-dust friend, which I deserve more than ever now.

I am tired. So fucking tired.

I let him in …

37

The painful strike into my genitalia wakes me. Murat is already on top of me, treating his morning erection with my dry, still-sleeping pussy. I groan and close my eyes again – it is too late for me to object and insist on him wearing a condom anyway. I turn my gloomy face away from his smelly morning breath, trying to brush away my thoughts of last night's surrender, which are not helping to cheer up the morning.

The stream of warm sperm that sprinkles all over my belly interrupts me from bitching at myself and finally frees me from Murat's heavy weight.

Thank God he is at least thoughtful enough not to come inside me.

He jumps up off the bed, too energetically for a person who's consumed and fucked for most of the night – I can't even lift my eyelids.

'Get up, Victoria!' His voice wakes me up. I probably fell asleep again without even wiping the now dried come off my body. 'There's coffee on the table. Please hurry up, beautiful, I have to go to work.'

Fifteen minutes later I am sitting in a taxi on the way home with $200 ($75 of which belongs to my pimp), a dry mouth that tastes like I have being drinking vinegar all night, and an agonising conscience that sours the taste in my mouth even more disgustingly.

When I get back home, Inna is still sleeping. I take a quick shower and quietly crawl under the blanket, grabbing her computer. I open my mailbox and find an email from Lena.

> Hi my little Poppy-seed ☺
> How are you doing? Hope everything is going well with you. ☺

A warm, silent stream of tears covers my cheeks. I stop reading to wipe them off. I feel so lonely and vulnerable. It has been only four days, but it feels like I've been gone for ages.

> We finally received our contracts from France and are ready to go to the embassy. Next week we are off to Kiev to do the applications. It shouldn't

take more than a day or two. As soon as we get
our visas, we are flying to Paris, and then going to
Nimes in the south of France by train.

The business is picking up. Nata and I are
advertising the salon. For the last three days
we've been giving out brochures on the streets
for a 10 per cent discount on all kinds of haircuts.
We've handed out close to a thousand each! I
feel exhausted, but you know our big sister, she
wouldn't get off my back until we were done. ☺

Mom is getting used to being a 'big boss' and
now she can take care of almost everything on her
own. Fast learner! Not like me. ☺

I am so excited about the France trip and so sad
you are not coming with us. We all miss you. Please,
please, please be careful – and email me as often as
you can!

Love you xxx

I quickly type a short reply, saying that I am fine and
miss all of them very much too, and drift off into a
deep but troubled sleep.

38

Alexandra was right. I am quite a busy call girl. Thin and blonde – nothing else matters! For some reason, Turkish men love to fuck skinny, bleached women, regardless of their boob size or looks.

So here I am, after two weeks of elbow grease, still in my pajamas at 4 p.m., sitting on the bed and counting how much money I've made so far. Inna is out on duty – our whoremaster-employer phoned her two hours ago. She quickly geared up and left. It feels so comfortingly pleasant to have the place to myself for a few hours. I enjoy these moments of privacy and even loneliness a lot – I can soak myself in my thoughts as much as I want.

For the last two weeks, I've been hired every single night; plus, once in a while Alexandra gave me a day job too, which I hate as much as I hated the Luxembourg day shift. The sunlight customers, as usual, are mostly boring, married guys who need a quickie and who are never up for the consumption of stimulants during their sessions.

Of course, I like the night calls more. They always involve booze and, quite often, drugs. From time to time I love to have a little bit of white powder – it makes me feel more confident, lulls my anxiety, and sometimes even encourages my horniness. It helps me to handle those dull or I-cannot-come-for-hours fuckers more easily. The only problem that I bump into every time is that as soon as the blow appears, I become much more compliant, and if the client is very persistent, I often agree to sex without protection. I've found a very stupid way of dealing with this problem: I do not think about it.

Yes! Latex-free intercourse is a common feature of the local clientele. Damn it! Every time, all sense of this being a highly civilised country slams into 'Aşkım, you can trust me. I am clean. Let's not use a rubber – I hate it!' This collision makes me feel like I am working in the middle of wild Africa.

Also, what is with the fucking-for-hours thing? In my short but quite experienced career, I've never met so many men in one place who struggle through rushed convulsions for hours each time they want to come.

In Inna's opinion, it has something to do with circumcision. 'I think the absence of the foreskin on the head of the penis – unlike members left in a primordial state – exposes it to unnecessary friction. With time, it loses its sensitivity.' My roommate pulls her favourite I-am-so-smart expression. 'First I thought it was a coincidence, but then I realised that I've fucked too many men in this city to consider it my ill fortune.'

I nodded, wondering where Inna gets all these theories, and tried to joke. 'I think this annoying problem has a simpler explanation. Maybe they just like to masturbate too much?'

On the other hand, the lack of perversion among Turkish guys – with the exception of the creepy yogi, and unlike my almost daily Luxembourg experience – is really helping to reduce my stress and tension during working hours. Most of the time, Turkish guys prefer straightforward sex in traditional positions.

In my two weeks here I've had only one case of the routine being different – I had a threesome. Alexandra sent me with another girl to join two young guys for a couple of hours. They were having a good time with booze and dope. The only thing missing was a duo of sexy girls. Sadly for my co-worker, neither of them liked her, even though they were both pretty hammered. So they apologised, gave her money for the cab and sent her back.

This can be unpleasant, but it's not the end of the world. All call girls are rejected once in a while.

The moment my teammate left, one of the guys called my pimp to ask for a replacement. Alexandra apologised, explaining that it was a weekend and all the girls were busy, and promised to send somebody as soon as possible.

We decided to wait a little while drinking, smoking green goddess, talking and laughing a lot. Then my clients left the room, 'to have a word with each other', as they put it. When they returned, they timidly explained that they both liked me, and asked if I wouldn't mind fucking both of them. Either because I was already quite smashed, or because the guys were really fun, the idea didn't seem that bad at all, and I agreed. As a result, we ended up performing all sorts of sandwiches in the fusion of drugs, fun, and lust.

So, after two weeks of intensive whoredom in Istanbul, I've made $1,560. Of course I want to make more, but I am not disappointed.

I am not feeling used and have nothing to complain about. It is my choice to do what I am doing. I could choose another route, like most of my schoolmates: enter the Kherson State Pedagogical University and go to work in a school, teaching history or Russian literature. Of course, one salary would not be enough for me to live a decent life. No matter how many extra hours I'd work or private lessons I'd give, there would still be days when I would go shopping for some basics like food or clothes, and would have to choose the tights over the kilogram of bananas because I wouldn't be able to afford both. Eventually, I would get married to some decent husband, not because I'd be madly in love with him, but simply because our union would hopefully help us both to pay the rent or make our lives more affordable.

No, this is not the way I want my life to be. My situation is not the model of perfect living, but at least it is a realistic attempt to grab a chance to improve things.

The lively melody of my cellphone interrupts my thinking. I see Alexandra's name on the display.

39

It is about ten o'clock in the evening. I am standing at the front desk of a very fancy residential building in Şişli. Inside and out it looks like a luxury hotel, the only difference being that these are fully serviced apartments instead of rooms and suites. I am waiting for the receptionist to check if I am an invited guest. He nods a few times into the receiver, then shows me the way to the elevator.

'Floor seven, madam.'

I smile my thanks at him, and head towards the wide, shiny elevator doors. Inside there are predictable full-length mirrors. I take in my reflection critically, trying to judge my appearance as objectively as I possibly can. My fairly pretty face is enhanced with skillful make-up (something good and useful, at least, from my friendship with Masha – all her life she suffered from a fear that she didn't look feminine enough, so she mastered the art of war-paint perfection). My wavy blonde hair flows down my shoulders. I'm in a modest, chic outfit – short-sleeved, light-blue blouse, knee-length flared white chiffon skirt, and some elegant silver high-heeled sandals that are high, but not overdone. I look sexy, but without the candid 'I AM A UKRAINIAN WHORE' look. I hate those I-know-who-you-are-and-why-you-are-here looks of the staff and guests of these hotels, and try to make sure that each time I cross another lobby, I at least plant a seed of doubt in those minds and make it harder for them to draw such conclusions. I'm happy with the reflection in the mirror, except for the obvious weariness in my eyes.

I look and feel exhausted! No wonder – it is my third call for today.

First, Alexandra woke me up in the afternoon from a comatose sleep resulting from last night's job, which I'd generously supplemented with some heavy consumption.

'Victoria, I have a job for you. Özgür from Ortaköy – I'm sure you remember him. He will be waiting for you in the same place as last time, at 3 p.m.'

I switched autopilot mode on and threw myself into a cold shower. It always worked – at 3:10 p.m. I was at the required destination.

Özgür was a ringed creature who was quick to come, always while wearing a condom, and generous to tip. To put it differently – a model client.

My 5 p.m. also wasn't bad, but the emptor lay on his back like a cripple on the bed, inducing me to spur him on to a gallop for the whole, endless hour.

At 7:30 p.m. I got back home, took a shower, and had dinner. As soon as I'd comforted myself with the remote control and a bottle of beer on the bed, my phone buzzed again.

Trick number three turns out to be no older than 25 and answers to the name of Ali. He is a short youngster, although well-built. He is definitely a regular in one of the local gyms.

I don't even look at his face until he hands me a glass of whisky on the rocks.

Wow …

His big, dark-brown eyes are charming and very naughty. He gazes into my eyes with a delightful and genuine smile, revealing a set of perfect white teeth. Apart from the looks, it is his sensational confidence that makes him a truly attractive man.

Hmmm … interesting …

I quickly scan the dwelling: huge, open-plan lounge with modern furniture and up-to-date gadgets. It looks like there is only one bedroom, so he definitely does not live with his parents. I also try to spot something to suggest a live-in girlfriend, wife or any other permanent fuck-mate, but fail to find anything – it is a typical bachelor's lair.

Okay ... let's take the rose-tinted glasses off and think rationally about this. He is handsome, young, attractive, confident and rich. There's got to be something wrong with him. What is it? A small dick? Some kind of perversion?

'You look tired, Victoria,' he murmurs, his voice full of genuine concern.

He is kind as well! Seriously – what's wrong with this one? He can't be this faultless. What's it going to be?

I shake my head energetically. 'No, not at all, I feel great, but thanks for asking.' I try to add as much get-up-and-go to my expression as I can. He smiles again and requests me to take a seat on his stunning white couch. It's in front of an enormous flat-screen TV that hangs on the wall. There's an unusually designed white glass coffee table between them.

'I have something more serious for you.' He pulls a little plastic bag of white powder from his pants pocket. 'I hope you will join me.'

Oh my fuck, he is perfect! It's my lucky day ...

Questions about what he does, or how he achieved all of this – especially considering his age – begin to climb into my curious brain. And I guess my face does not want to work with me, making my thoughts clear as a bell instead, as if they were written on my forehead …

'No, I am not a successful businessman, or some talented artist … I am an average student in the Faculty of Architecture at Bosphorus University. For all of this –' his eyes take a trip around the room '– I have my parents to thank. Fortunately or unfortunately for me, my mom and dad are wealthy people who love me and spoil me a lot.' I pick up the sorrow in his words.

I sniff a juicy line with cold neutrality on my face while nodding vaguely. I always feel confused, angry even, when the rich and spoiled fish for sympathy about their lives that are 'so hard'.

The next question that begins to bug me even more is why the hell would he call Alexandra in the first place?

'I am not doing this because I need to pay for sex.'

Damn! What is it tonight? Is he some kind of psychic, or is it my face that keeps failing to cooperate with me?

'I just like beautiful, intelligent and sexy women … women like you, who don't think of sex as a duty they have to perform to reproduce. I mean, I like to be with a woman who sees lovemaking as a great gift that we, as humans, are blessed to enjoy. But, unfortunately, most women I meet just use sex as a

tool that helps them to get married; or even worse –
they are ashamed of it, as if it is something dirty.'

I try hard to concentrate on what Ali is saying, but
the tender touch of his fingers, which play with my
neck while lightly tousling my hair, makes my skin
prickle and my brain freeze.

He is wearing a white T-shirt, loose light-blue
jeans, and nothing on his feet. One of his legs is
folded under his thigh and the foot of the other is
feeling the wood of the floors. It is sexy … everything
about him is extremely sexy, composed, seductive.

Ali leans forward. Without touching my body, he
kisses me, passionately sucking and biting my lips.

Oh my … he is good …

*No, no, no … what is it? Is he a mutant with two
dicks? Or … is his tool missing? I wonder which of these
would upset me more …*

He stops abruptly and relaxes back, placing his
arm again on the top of the couch so he can go back
to playing with my neck. I sigh but don't open my
eyes, trying to prolong the unreal lust into which my
whole body has just dived. It feels so heavenly and
intense down my stomach. Eventually I open them.
Ali is watching me with a contented smile on his face.

'Have a drink, beautiful.' His voice is calm and
comforting. 'Tell me more about yourself, your
childhood?'

I begin the story about my sisters and their trip
to France, which I couldn't take with them; and how

my friend Inna, who I bumped into about a month ago, is the reason for my being in Istanbul. He keeps asking leading questions, demonstrating his deep interest in my tale, pressing me for more details.

Without taking his eyes off my face, he slowly starts undoing the small pearly-blue buttons on my blouse, and pulls my bra cups slightly down, just enough to get better access to my nipples. He starts playing with them.

I automatically reach my arm out towards him, to answer his arousing strokes. Ali stops me, gently replacing my hand. 'Don't, beautiful … please continue … you were saying?'

No one has ever done anything like this to me before. Usually my sex-mates, clients or boyfriends lose interest in my boobies quickly, after a few squeezes and rubs. Men ignore them throughout intercourse, seeking compensation in the other parts of my body. Because of this lack of stimulation, I didn't even know that my nipples were erogenous zones, capable of discharging so much warmth down to my crotch.

I understand that me talking at the same time as being stimulated so strongly is a part of Ali's game. He gives me a simple task – to entertain him with some tales – and watches me fail to do it, because of the desire that fills up my body and mind. It's pure amusement for him to see how, with only a few touches, he has changed me into his horny puppet.

Without a doubt he can call the night a success, because my face is red, my voice becomes hoarse, my pulse and breathing quicken and all of my body tenses in its obvious plea to be fucked.

Some time later, when it turns into insanity and my pussy is swallowed in desire, and the only thing left in my entire world is how I'm dying for satisfaction, he slowly starts undoing his jeans. Next thing, he is tearing apart the foil of the condom. He rolls it over his not very long but thick and promisingly firm member.

My legs open slightly in irrepressible anticipation. My mouth opens to inhale deeply.

'Lift up your skirt, beautiful. I want to see how much you want my cock inside you.' I follow his instruction and reveal my splashing slit.

'Good girl. Come here. Let's see what I can do for you.' He smiles, drags me up and places me on top of him. Then, tightly grasping both of my wrists behind my back with one hand, he searches through the layers of my skirt with the other, moves my panties to one side, grabs my ass, and nails me on his erection.

The flash of disappointment at being on top again dissolves in a loud, wild sound that breaks out of my throat, echoing the powerful wave of inconceivable pleasure that pierces my whole body, violently smashes into me, and scatters to my limbs like a million butterflies.

He straightens his back, making it easier for him to move me, control the rhythm, and suck and bite my nipples while keeping my hands still. One strike after another. Until I collapse.

40

For the next couple of days all I can think of is that night. It could hardly even be called a night – unfortunately it was over soon after I hit my really big O. But it was *the* night because of the divine sex I had with an awesome guy while consuming a perfect amount of the good stuff.

After I came, Ali didn't give me much time to recover. My vagina was still convulsing when he brusquely lifted me up and put me back onto my weak, shaky legs behind the conveniently tall and wide armrest of the couch. Then he bent me over, throwing the white chiffon of my skirt over my head, and tugged my panties down to my knees.

'Hold your butt cheeks with both your hands, beautiful, and do not let them go …' His voice sounded calm but extremely demanding. I complied, shifting my feet, trying to get more sureness in my position. 'Stay still and do not let them go,' he repeated, with more affection this time, and forcefully penetrated me.

He fucked me hard while pulling back my hair, which he'd tied in his fist, saying over and over, 'Don't let your hands go, my angel. Good girl …' until he came loudly, making me scream too from how he painfully pulled my hair even more …

Then he brought some wet wipes from the bathroom, apologetically explained that the next day he had very early classes and had to get some sleep, paid my fees, and showed me to the door.

That night was not only the best sexual experience I'd ever had, it was the only time I'd ever climaxed with a man inside me. Its not like I don't know what an orgasm feels like; I've been a big fan of masturbation since I was thirteen. I'd been pleasuring myself almost every day, in the shower or in bed before going to sleep. Even zonked out Inna under the same blanket never stopped me. I grew up with two sisters, sharing one room, and I got used to them being a silent and non-participative presence while I was busy flying to another Promised Land.

Hmmm ... coming with Ali felt so different. I guess that was what they call hitting the G-spot or a vaginal orgasm.

The sexual desire that built up and filled my body with the power of an avalanche during his foreplay was as frighteningly good as it was surprisingly intense for me too. I could never have suspected that my body was capable of that feeling. But when Ali started shoving me down on his cock, I simply lost it ... The inner hit that stormed every inch of my insides dissolved my body, crushing me into countless colourful lights, like a 4th of July discharged firework.

I close my eyes, trying to recall the sensation again and again ... damn, it was good. I need it. Every minute I hope my phone will start ringing, and that it will be Alexandra, whose soft, seductive voice would say, 'Victoria, do you remember that client from Şişli? He wants you back.'

Oh my! That would be so great ...

The phone does ring. It's Alexandra. 'Hey Victoria, how are you? I have a job for you. It's a new client; he wants you to come to Asia side, so start getting ready now. He will be waiting for you in two hours.'

Crap.

41

Another month disappears. It whisks by in a haze: I'm constantly drowning in booze and drugs, or in a deep sleep to get over the booze and drugs.

I am sitting in our kitchen, having my 'morning' coffee and cigarette at 3 p.m. and checking my inbox, ignoring naked Inna, who hurriedly runs in and out of the bathroom. She is gearing up; there is a client waiting for her in an hour's time.

Hi my Poppy-seed,
How are you? Hope everything is going well with you in Istanbul … I can't believe we're apart, and that Natalia and I can't keep an eye on you.

We are finally in Nimes. We had a good flight and an easy switch to the train in Paris. It is unbelievably fast. We crossed all of France just in three hours!

When we got here, the owner of the club, his name is Paul, met us at the station and took us to the apartment. He looks like a nice chap; although he is ex-military and he doesn't speak English at all!

So after all, the trip was good, except for the incident at the French embassy in Kiev. Oh my! Those bastards treat people like complete garbage!

You remember our trip to the Luxembourgish embassy in Moscow? That fat bitch who almost killed me, threatening to reject my application because I used the bathroom? Yes, I know it said 'Staff Only', but it was the only loo they had. What I was supposed to do?

This time it was quite a young man who submitted our papers for the visa. He just started yelling at Natalia and I because we whispered a few words and smiled at each other while he was busy checking our contracts and certificates. Besides, this place didn't even have a bathroom, regardless of the fact that we had to spend three hours there ...

Anyway, what doesn't kill us will make us stronger, right?

The club looks very small – we just had a tour with Paul. The apartments we stay in are awesome.

It's a double-storey, spacious, holiday-style flat with an open-plan kitchen.

Okay, Jul, I have to run, still have to unpack, shower and get ready to work. It's our first night, and I am so scared now ... Natalia looks cool as a cucumber though! You know she is an 'iron lady' ☺! Write me about what is happening on your side? How is business? How is Inna doing?

We miss you very much.

xxx

'What the fuck is this, Jul? Have you totally sniffed your brains out?'

Inna's angry yell shakes me up with fright. I look up from the computer screen. Still undressed, now wearing only a tiny black G-string and high heels, she is standing in the middle of the room with a small plastic bag, stuffed with white powder, in her hand.

'What the fuck are you thinking?' Her voice gets even louder.

'What is your problem? Stop shouting! You scared the shit out of me! You get wasted all the time too, with the only difference being that your fuel is liquid! So why don't you just address some of those questions to yourself?'

'I don't care what you do out there, but I don't want this shit in my place! Don't you understand that there is a huge difference between being deported because they drag you off the client, and getting yourself thrown into jail because you carry your weekly stock with you?' She lowers the volume.

I stay silent; I have nothing to say to Inna. I am offended by her tone but she is right.

She sighs and takes few steps closer to the table, still waving the little plastic bag in the air.

'Look. I know we all like to have some fun while doing the "best job in the world", but I beg you not to bring this stuff in here anymore, okay? I heard there were quite a few police raids in Laleli and Aksaray yesterday. They storm the hotels, drag the girls out of their beds and throw them into jail. Without even seeing them on a customer! Do you get it, Jul?! The cops have started to play really dirty. You never know … we could even get reported by one of our friendly but fucking curious neighbours and then we will get fucked for real …'

I nod.

'Okay, I need to go now. I am sorry I shouted at you, but I am really scared of getting into trouble, especially over bullshit stuff like this.'

42

Inna and I are packing to go home for a couple of days. Our sixty-day tourist visas expire tomorrow and we have to cross the border to get new ones, for another two months.

This time I convince my roommate to take a plane. I can't even think of locking myself on that boat again. Besides, I can take no gear with me. It's obviously too dangerous to carry drugs across the border. That means at least 48 hours without a hit or a drag of dope. I have to be creative. I check, and find only two possible routes: through Odessa or Nikolayev.

The latter is closer to Kherson and is cheaper as well – looks like a real catch for us. An hour-and-a-half flight, then another hour on the bus, and we are home. It's a charter flight, An-24, and once a week it goes to Istanbul from Nikolayev and back. Since the end of the Soviet era in the late 80s, the air transport system, including most of the government-owned airports, has been neglected, especially in the little towns, to the point of complete dysfunction. For the last few years, this has been the only flight that's landed at and taken off from Nikolayev International Airport.

I was optimistic, thinking that nothing could be worse than two days on a thirty-year-old boat full of passengers and at least half of the crew who were hammered into a critical condition.

I was mistaken …

The first thing that shocks us is the size of the airplane. It looks more like a bus with propellers and wings. Then we learn that smoking is permitted onboard – anyone who wishes to have a drag can go to the cargo section at the end of the aircraft and enjoy a cigarette.

Faster and safer …? Hmm … I guess the only thing I didn't slip up with is the 'faster' part – this definitely looks to me like a pretty fast way of kicking the bucket.

Despite this, the flight to Nikolayev goes well and we get home in one piece. Two days go by very quickly. Before I know it I am in a cab, going to fetch Inna on the way to Nikolayev to fly back to Istanbul.

As we arrive and head for the check-in, the woman at the counter looks at our itinerary and says that there are some problems; before she can issue our boarding passes we have to go to the office to sort them out.

Inna and I exchange annoyed looks and without any further comments head up the stairs, following the woman's directions. There are at least another seven already stressed passengers waiting in the reception area. From their conversation, we learn that the airline has overbooked the flight by selling at least ten extra tickets; now they are trying to decide who to leave behind.

Unfuckingbelievable! Classic bullshit!

We finally get approached by one of the airline staff. A short, ball-shaped woman with ridiculous combed-back blonde hair, who looks as if she went to sleep in the 70s, stayed in a heavy slumber for 30 years and, for some unknown-to-mankind reason, woke up this morning, forgot to look in the mirror and came to work.

'There was a mistake in the system and the flight is overbooked. I am very sorry. We are trying to do everything possible to fix that, but it's the airline's decision that the passengers who paid for their tickets in Ukraine are first in the line to get on board.'

'Bullshit!' This was not Inna talking; it was the spirit of the six-pack of beers she'd guzzled in the cab on the way to the airport, complaining that she was scared of flying. 'It's unacceptable! We've paid for our fucking tickets! No matter where we did so, we have the right to be treated the same way as others!' Inna is already screaming while looking down at the teased white mop. It is clear that Inna is about to lose it for real. The woman takes a small step back and starts babbling, 'Don't worry, girls. I will make sure you get on this flight.'

While tipsy, Inna is trying to explain to the woman how unfair it is when people get divided, and that this is pure discrimination, and while the woman in turn struggles to calm Inna down, I overhear a conversation between the check-in staff we saw earlier and one of the crew members. Turns out that the airline has decided to take all 60 passengers instead of 50, to make more money. The flight is also very much overloaded, exceeding its cargo weight allowance.

What the hell? Why can't I just find an inexpensive but civilised way of traveling?

I freak out but decide not to tell Inna – no one knows how she will react to this piece of information.

As we get checked in and go through security and passport control, we walk into the waiting area, which has a funny sign – 'Накопитель' – on its entry door. I am sure that this white and blue board has been there since Soviet times, and I find it quite difficult to translate or explain to the part of the world that doesn't speak Russian. Instead of simply naming the waiting area 'waiting area' or 'departure lounge', the sign says 'Accumulator', meaning that the area was designed to gather travellers before boarding. But the nature of the word and its usage gives the passengers a feeling that they are not humans, but a flock of sheep that needs to be restrained.

It has such a communistic flavour – 'From each according to his abilities, to each according to his needs[22]'. But it always happened that people's needs were reduced to the point of absurdity. For instance, when the rest of the world had been using Pampers since 1961, the greatest and the most powerful country in the world wouldn't even consider producing a similar item. To make its people's lives better or more comfortable was never a part of Soviet policy. Up until the end of the 90s, we were using swaddling clothes or napkins.

Same story here … the preposterous sign leads to the waiting area filled with uncomfortable and half-broken wooden chairs, dirty toilets, and a dodgy kiosk selling cheap vodka and instant swill that can hardly be called coffee, both served in awful plastic cups.

Classic!

22 Karl Marx, *The Critique of the Gotha Program*

This attitude touched every aspect of people's lives. The level of technological development, including utilities for the home like washing machines, dishwashers or microwaves, medicine, and the auto industry, was low and shamefully backward. Nothing was ever done to improve the living conditions of the regular Soviet citizen, because it was always assumed that he or she needed basics and nothing more.

The word 'Накопитель' on the doors of the waiting area is a perfect example of the quality of life that we Soviet folk had through all those years. We were brainwashed puppets, who actually believed that our country was the best in the world, and that it gave us the best living conditions possible … ever!

Arggh … pathetic …

Nevertheless, it was not the end of our shocking trip; the low point was the actual boarding. The procedure is different from anything you've ever experienced before: the passengers walk across the apron to the aircraft, carrying their own luggage. As they approach the plane, they have to lift their bags and pass them to the man in the cargo section. And now for the best part: imagine this process when all the travellers know that there are ten fewer seats on the plane than the number of people about to board. Ha! Unforgettable scene! As soon as the ground crew leads us out of the building, all the passengers (excluding Inna and me, of course) start a race to get a seat.

Oh my fuck!

Inna and I continue walking, experiencing a culture shock. 'What's wrong with these people?' I can hear from Inna's voice that she's quickly sobered up. 'Are we in a war zone or something?' She continues her comments while pulling her luggage through the thick, tall grass. We are the last to get on board. Sweating after the walk and the battle with our bags (the cargo door was higher than our heads), we finally get on board.

'Can I see your boarding passes?' the young flight attendant approaches us with a welcoming smile and confusion in her eyes. 'I am sorry – there are no more seats available ...'

'We can see that,' Inna interrupts, calmly, but with a hopping-mad expression on her face. 'Shall we make ourselves comfortable on the wing?'

It's funny, but no one smiles.

'Would you mind going to the cockpit? Unfortunately it has only one folding seat, but you could share, and the flight is only an hour and a half. I am really sorry for the inconvenience.'

'Fantastic!' Inna throws, and heads to the front. As we walk down the aisle, we notice that some people are sitting on each other's laps, while a few have settled themselves on the floor near the toilet at the back.

Despite all this, the flight goes smoothly and we get to Istanbul safely.

Alleluia!

43

I switch on my cellphone to a text from Alexandra. 'I believe you are back, girls. I will need both of you tonight. Call me back as soon as you can.' I show it to Inna, who frowns, lights a cigarette, and mumbles, 'Back to work …'

We rush back home, swallow some take-aways that we grab on the way, and jump into the shower. A few minutes before leaving our apartment, I get another text from our pimp with the client's name and address.

I can't believe my eyes – it is Ali's address! The name is different, though. The blood rushes through my head and my heart is jumping out of my chest. *Oh my fuck! Please, please, please ... let it be him ...*

The concierge is the same man, but I doubt he recognises me. The unpleasant thought about how many women Ali has fucked since our first session leaves a sour taste in my mouth. But the front door thrown open immediately after we buzz banishes my navel-gazing: it's him ...

'Hi girls, you are right on time!' he almost shouts through the ear-piercing music with his delicious smile, the image of which I'd carefully stored in my memory's 'forever' file after I first met him.

'Please come on in!'

The music is so loud we don't even bother to respond.

I can see the pleasant surprise on Inna's face; I don't know whether it's about the design of the apartment or our host.

The light in the living room is dimmed. The white designer coffee table, illuminated by the TV's flashing light, is stuffed with liqueur bottles, packets of chips, cigarettes, and a beautifully adorned silver tray of white powder.

Inna and I settle on the couch. The guys are already pretty tipsy. While organising us some drinks, they explain the occasion.

'This is my best buddy, Ersin,' Ali utters with a smile, fondly squeezing and shaking Ersin's shoulders, 'and today is his birthday! So you ladies will help me make it a really special night for him.'

They both giggle, and before I know it, Ersin drops onto the couch next to me, handing me a glass of bubbly, while Ali settles next to Inna.

The pulse in my head starts painfully to strike – either Ali is so drunk that he doesn't even recognise me, or his friend liked me more than Inna and he is just too much of a gentleman to spoil Ersin's birthday present.

Crap! I sound like Lena already ...

The next thing I see is Inna and Ali smooching and groping each other. And before I even get the picture, Ersin is pulling me into the bedroom ...

The birthday boy takes off his jeans, pulls off my top, and, after a few kisses and grabs of my nipples, puts me down on my knees and pushes his hard cock into my mouth. 'Suck it, baby. I want to come in your mouth.'

I do as I'm told, like a zombie. The jealousy drowns me in rage and hurt; all I can hear are Inna's loud sex breaths and screams in the next room.

'You are not in the mood?' Ersin asks me while lifting me up off the floor and throwing me on the bed. Then he climbs on top and fucks me until he comes. An unstoppable hot stream of tears runs down my face, which I don't even try to wipe or hide. I don't care about anything but those noises. Ersin doesn't notice them anyway until the moment he rolls off me. 'Oh … you liked it too …' he says with a satisfied smile. 'It's okay, don't worry, I've seen that before – your tears are from the strong orgasm you just experienced …'

Swollen-headed idiot!

We wait for some time, until the other room goes quiet, then we dress and walk out. Ali is lying on the couch wearing only boxers; Inna, naked, picks up her clothes and goes to the bathroom. I can't look at them. I am scared I will start crying again right there, in front of him.

Ersin takes my hand and pulls me to the couch, makes me sit down, gives Ali five and exclaims, 'Wow, buddy, the best birthday present ever!' They both start laughing.

Inna comes back all dressed, pours herself another glass and addresses me with a smile: 'Are we all paid and ready to go, Victoria?'

Ali gets up and searches in his pants pocket for the money, then hands it to me.

'Victoria, I will give you an extra fifty if you say now that I was a better lover than him.'

They start laughing loud again, and Inna exclaims, surprised, 'What are you talking about? I didn't know you two knew each other?'

All I can feel are the pulsing strikes in my head and the hot tears on my lips again. 'Fuck you!' I throw the money into Ali's face and storm out of the door.

'What the hell happened there?' Inna's stunned voice is almost screaming when, a few minutes later, she finds me sitting and crying on the sidewalk in the parking lot behind the building.

'Are you insane? Why did you throw the money at him?'

I say nothing and she hunkers down in front of me, removing my hands from my tear-stained face. 'What's wrong, baby? Talk to me …'

'Don't you get it? I daydream about this bastard for the whole month but he chooses you!' A new stream of blubbering muffles the end of my sentence.

'If I'd known you knew him and had feelings for him, I would never have done anything like that,' Inna exclaims. 'I am sorry, Jul, I wish I'd known … Why didn't you tell me?'

'When I realised that the bastard didn't even recognise me it was too late. Besides, what could I say? It was clear he wanted to fuck you …'

'Okay, Jul. Let's find a cab and get out of here.'

She gets up and pulls me up too.

'Please don't cry. He is a jerk!'

She sighs and hugs my shoulders.

'Although I completely understand why you were so carried away by him. He is a great fuck … But Jul, you are not sixteen any more. You can't act like you are, and because of bullshit like this throw away the money we work so hard to earn.'

'I know. I'm sorry. I just lost it ...' I reply, feeling guilty.

'You know what?' Inna smiles to me as we get into the cab. 'Let's stop at the grocer on the way home and get some cheesecake and ice cream. It's the best panacea for any love-related blues, and luckily does not require a prescription.'

'I am not in love, Inna! What nonsense!' I protest with a weak smile.

Then why the hell I am so attached and emotional? I've only seen this guy twice in my life but I've never felt anything like this before?

When we get home, we take a quick shower, jump into bed, drink some wine, eat our asses off, watch some Russian comedy that Inna chose 'to help the healing process', and fall asleep.

44

The melody of my cell phone wakes me up. Although it feels early, I assume it's at least midday.

'Hello,' I answer, without even looking at the number, trying to clear my throat at the same time. The noise that comes out of me makes me sound more like an ogre than a 19-year-old, 49 kilogram woman.

'Hello ... Victoria? Can I speak to Victoria, please?' The voice makes me jump off the bed.

'Yes, it's Victoria speaking.' I sound a little better and he recognises me. 'It's Ali ... from last night. Please don't put the phone down. I know you are upset with me but that's why I'm calling you.' He hesitates for a second. 'I found your number in my cellphone. If you remember, you called me for directions the first time we met, a month ago.'

He pauses and I stay quiet too. My heart beats so loudly that I am scared he will hear it.

'I wanted to apologise for what happened last night. I acted like a jerk ... I guess. I didn't know I was hurting your feelings.'

'No worries, even though you did act like a jerk. Apology accepted.' I try to talk without my voice getting neurotically squeaky. 'Anything else?'

'Yes. I was wondering if you would give me a chance to apologise in person. Would you consider having a dinner with me?'

'Yes, I would.' Damn. I answer too quickly and my voice does squeak.

'How about tonight? Are you available?' I can hear him smiling on other side of the line.

'Okay!' Damn my voice again!

'Alrighty then, great. I will see you around eight?' I hear relief in his voice too, so despite his un-fucking-imaginable confidence he was nervous about calling me.

'Okay, great. Let me know where.' And I hang up.

'Why are you smiling?' Inna is standing in front of me.

I put my phone down and figure I have a stupid I-am-in-love expression on my face that is absolutely uncontrollable at this point.

I switch on the kettle, trying to wipe the stupidity off my face, but it seems it's not working.

'Ali called and invited me for dinner!' Now I sound like an out-of-tune violin in the hands of a five-year-old.

Inna takes a seat on the kitchen stool. 'Look, Jul, like I said, you are not a schoolgirl any more and you know what to do, but I feel like I have to warn you anyway.' She pauses. 'I am not a mentalist, but from what I've seen of Ali, I can assure you, he is not good for you. I especially wouldn't trust a man who uses drugs. You are going to get hurt.'

She pauses again, this time waiting for me to respond, but I stay silent.

'I am not your mom,' she continues, with a more annoying concerned look on her face, 'and don't want to lecture you …'

'So don't!' I rudely interrupt her and get two cups from the cupboard.

'Okay, Jul, do what you want to. Just don't say I didn't warn you.' She heads to the bathroom.

I snap 'Whatever' at her and quickly type a text to Alexandra saying that I am not feeling well, so she mustn't count on me tonight.

Hi my Poppy-seed,
I was happy to get your letter today ☺! Don't be lazy Jul. Write to me more often. You know we miss you and worry about you a lot ☺

Our first night here was a complete disaster!

Just before the shift our boss gave us instructions about the rules of the club, repeating that it's an absolutely sex-free zone (by the way, totally in French ☺). Then a few hours later, while I was sitting at the bar a few steps away from him and Melissa, our barwoman, I opened my purse to get a tissue – and a pack of condoms fell out onto the floor. Our boss, as a real gentleman, quickly leaned down to pick up what I had just lost. Oh my ... you should have seen his face ☺!

Of course I took condoms to work. In Luxembourg we had the same instructions, and it turned out that the only way we could make money was by fucking. Who the hell knew that this time they actually meant it?! The man was furious and lectured me for an hour at least in his office, talking to me as if I was a soldier at fault in some field of operations. Anyway, it's all good now ☺.

Okay, need to run – going shopping with Nata. Don't be a stranger, Jul. Waiting for your letters ☺. Love you lots ...

xxx

45

A few more text messages from Ali and we've set a time and place. He insists on having dinner at his place, explaining that he is an excellent cook:

> I am going to blow your mind with my signature three-cheese fondue, for which I have a perfect bottle of Bordeaux ☺ x

I screw up my face, still feeling the heaviness in my head from last night, and text him back:

> I have no doubt you will blow my mind, and trust me, the food is the last thing I am thinking about when I say that ☺ x

The reminder of why my head is falling apart today nudges me to go to the fridge and pull out a bottle of cold beer. A few gulps and I don't feel so shitty anymore – it is the best hair of the dog humanity has come up with yet.

I try to keep myself busy with cleaning and washing and deciding what to wear, but the day seems never-ending.

As I walk into Ali's apartment building, the memories of last night strike me, removing a lot of the anticipation and excitement in which I'd spent the whole day. He fucked Inna on his perfectly white leather couch … and they both enjoyed it …

Shit … Maybe dinner in his apartment was not such a good idea …

The front door is open. Michael Jackson belting out the unmistakable Billie Jean on the stereo makes it impossible for me to announce my presence. I spot the romantic dinner set up for two on the kitchen bar counter. It looks sweet: candles in wine glasses instead of the usual holders, a bunch of fresh violets in a short whisky glass instead of a vase, plates and cutlery. The sight makes me smile and I toss all those creepy memories of the previous night as far away as I can.

I walk in further and see Ali at the stove. I can't resist and start laughing. He is actually doing a little hip-hop dance while wearing an apron, mixing something very delicious in a saucepan and singing some of the lyrics badly, using a wooden spoon as a microphone.

'I would never have thought that you're a big fan of the King of Pop.'

He notices me, gives me his shy smile and turns the volume down.

'You are early? For how long have you been standing here, watching me?' He adds some playfully worried notes, 'If you've seen me moonwalking, I'll have to kill you.' He quickly kisses me on the lips and goes back to the stove.

'That was amusing. You shouldn't have stopped,' I tease and come closer to check what he's cooking. 'Smells delicious.'

'Wait until you try it … another five minutes and we are all set.'

Ali pours me a glass of wine, cuts some French baguette into small cubes and puts the pot with melted cheese on a special tray with a few candles underneath it, right next to a bowl of Greek-style salad on the table.

'Have you ever eaten fondue?'

I shake my head.

'Oh, well, there is not just eating involved. We are going to play a little game at the same time.' He smiles with such excitement, like a boy waiting at the Christmas tree knowing that in a few seconds he will be able to open his long-awaited presents.

I raise my eyebrows and smile back at him. 'A game?'

Jesting, he continues, 'The rules are simple, Victoria …'

'Call me Julia, please. It's my real name,' I interrupt him. 'Sorry, you were saying?'

'Hmmm …' Ali takes a sip from his glass, 'Julia … so much better than Victoria.' Then he smiles and adds a little bit more seriously, 'Thanks for sharing that … it means a lot to me.'

'My pleasure,' I quickly answer while hungrily looking at the pot.

He starts laughing. 'Shame, Julia, I didn't know you were that hungry! Let's start … I will explain how it works as we eat.'

He takes my fondue fork, pokes it into one of the bread cubes and dips it into the melted cheese. 'You see? It is very easy. Try …'

I bite it off the fork. 'Hmm … it is delicious! Hmmm … you are good …'

'If you carry on making those noises, I can't promise I will let you finish dinner, Julia.'

His voice makes my insides twist and I feel pleasant warmness down my belly.

Oh my fuck. He hasn't even touched me and I am already horny as hell.

'Hmm …' I tease him again, 'sounds promising. So, you wanted to tell me about the game?'

'Mainly, there is one rule: while we eat, we must
try not to lose our pieces of bread in the saucepan.
Whoever drops the most will have to comply with all
the wishes of the winner. In other words, the winner
is going to be the master tonight.'

As he speaks there is so much badness in his eyes
that I fidget on my stool, trying to calm my already-
burning-with-desire vagina.

'I am in. I'm liking this dinner more and more –
tasty and fun!' I say and let one piece of bread slip
back into the pot straight away. 'Oopsy!' I put on my
flirty-naughty face. 'It looks like I will end up very
hungry tonight ...'

Time goes by; the evening is lively and tasty. After
dinner, Ali suggests we move to the couch with the
wine to have some dessert. He points at the silver tray
with its coke that I hadn't noticed.

It can't get better than this ... seriously!

The rest of the night we spend sniffing and fucking
like crazy all over the place: on the tables, on the
floor, against the walls and in the shower. We get to
bed only at sunrise, with the first call to prayer.

As we lie spooning, exhausted and half asleep,
Ali plays with a lock of my hair and gently bites my
shoulder.

'You know, I am not a big fan of relationships and
commitment, but the honesty and courage in your
eyes when you threw the money at me last night

shook me somehow. I thought about you all night. Really, I couldn't sleep.' I hear the confusion in his voice.

'Yeah, I was stupid to do that,' I say and yawn at the same time.

I hear him smile. 'Okay, it was a little stupid, but there was so much bluntness in your act as well. Trust me, Julia, not many people are capable of that.'

'Uh huh.' I'm struggling to keep up, and fall asleep.

* * *

I wake up alone in the bed; the place is quiet. I check the time. It's 10 a.m. – Ali is probably at his lectures already. Wow. What a night – it was supernatural …

The swelling and slight discomfort in my pussy is the sweetest evidence that last night was not just a dream.

I jump into the shower, dress and go to the kitchen to make some coffee, while thoughtlessly singing 'I can't help falling in love' by UB40.

I find a note and two hundred-dollar bills on the kitchen table, next to the violets:

'It was a wonderful night. Thanks. Hope to see you soon … A.'

I smile, feeling fluttering butterflies in my chest, finish my coffee and leave without touching the money.

46

The next couple of weeks are really exhausting. I am fucked up. I can't stop thinking about him. When I sleep, I dream about him. When I am awake, everything around me reminds me of him, and that eats up all of my consciousness. When other men touch me, I experience an almost physical pain and I want to cry, because I wish they were him.

Even my body is in bad condition.

While Alexandra keeps me busy, giving me two or three jobs a day, I drown myself in gallons of liquor and mountains of coke to make the hours when I am consumed by other men go faster and less painfully. Keeping my head as misty as possible helps, but at the same time, my body is struggling to handle all the crap I take in to reach that state.

On the rare occasions when Ali has a break in his studies, I come up with another lie for Alexandra about a painful period, headache or high blood pressure, and we can spend another perfect night together. And still, I take in a lot of blow, because Ali likes to relax and I just don't know when to stop. As a result, I can hardly tell day from night. I often don't remember who I fucked yesterday, and don't really care who I'll be with tomorrow. I am tired, very tired, and the only emotion I am capable of right now is hatred for Alexandra and all the I-hate-condoms-and-love-to-fuck-for-hours clients she sends me to. There are so many of them; the fucking never ends. But I don't care … Ali … I wait for him to call me and tell me when we can meet again.

I don't know where are we going with this relationship, if you could even call it that. Ali feeds me with some bullshit excuse that he cannot commit to anything until he finishes his studies. 'It is something I promised to my parents and myself. Nothing will stop or distract me from getting a degree. First, a good job, then a family.'

Blah blah blah …

But I don't really care, as long as he lets me be with him at least sometimes. I get through three, four or sometimes five, six days and as many as ten, 15 or even 20 dicks knowing that I will see him again. That is all that matters.

Although, apparently I don't look okay anymore either, and get increasingly more comments from Inna about needing a rest. 'You must take a day off, Jul. You look very tired,' or 'If you do call in sick, stay in bed, you need to catch up on some sleep.'

Yes, I am very tired, but why can't you just shut up and mind your own business? I don't need your concern. If I get a chance to see him, I will.

I even stopped answering Inna, to save some energy on arguments. Or, it could be that I just don't care about anything but the following Friday. Ali told me he is going out with his friends for a boy's night out, but that if I want I could join him afterwards at his place.

Friday. I will see him on Friday …

Hi my Poppy-seed,

How are you doing?

You wouldn't believe what happened last night ☺! My Michel decided to surprise me and without saying a word showed up in our cabaret ☺! OMF! We opened six bottles of Dom Perignon and got wasted together with Natalia ☺. Obviously he drank most of it, and even needed assistance ☺☺☺ to get into a cab!

We had so much fun☺. It was a really great surprise …

What's more, our boss agreed to give me a day off today! I never thought that this short-sighted bumpkin was capable of humane actions like this ☺!

So we took the opportunity in full and went to some fancy place by the sea.

What's on your side? Don't forget to write back to me …

Love you my little sister ☺

xxx

47

He is in his mid-30s, well-built and very polite. So polite that it's creepy. My intuition is definitely trying to tell me something, but I don't listen. My brains are busy enjoying a deep dive in the warm river of the memories of the last night I spent with Ali.

Okay, it was not even a night ... When he called me it was already 3 a.m. He asked me to bring some coke. I got to his place at four. He fucked me crazily, as always, and then didn't let me stay there, because his parents were visiting him for breakfast. They wanted to check how he was doing with his 'independent life', for which they are still paying.

'Would you like some of this?' The man shows me a sealed little bag of coke, after bringing us two glasses of whisky. He is just friendly; nothing wrong with that. But when I look at his smiling face my heart sinks – there is something *very* not right in his eyes.

I try to calm myself down. Alexandra told me that even though I'd never worked with him before he is an old client she'd known for ages.

He sets up a few lines and watches me doing them, still wearing his creepy smile. I rub my nose, but instead of my usual feeling, my hunch gets obsessively bigger. He is weird, fucking weird ... *Why doesn't he sniff himself? Or if he doesn't do drugs why would he have them on him in the first place?*

But I stop myself, trying not to overthink the situation, keeping in mind that Alexandra knows the man, so he should be safe.

The creep is quite generous and asks if I would like another hit before we go to his bedroom. I don't say no and get loaded pretty well, ignoring my anxiety and diluting my consciousness in the mist I try to stay in.

We go to the bedroom and the fucking, for the most part, turns to harsh but standard. He bangs me with a condom, then some time later persuades me to take it off, promising another hit. I don't really know how much time has passed but it seems he's been perforating me for an extensive period already.

He is getting tired and frustrated.

'I want to fuck your ass, Sweetie,' he exclaims without stopping the digging.

'I don't do ass-fucking, sorry.' My answer is broken up by my breathing. 'Oh, come on. I'll give you a nice take-away.' He obviously means more drugs for me in exchange.

'Do you think I am a crack whore, or what?' I lose it and almost shout. 'Get off me!'

He doesn't move, his body weight pressing me even harder into the mattress. He smiles viciously. 'Hmm … you refuse, and resist me? That's even better!'

I try to push him off me as hard as I can, threatening to go to the police if he does not stop, but I can't do anything. He is at least twice as heavy as me, and we both know I can't go to the police.

He laughs back, throws me face-down on the pillow, locks my neck firmly with one hand and tries to hold me still while grabbing my ass with the other. After a short battle, he forces his hard cock into my anus.

I scream from a strike of burning pain.

This only encourages him to brutalise his assault, thrusting faster and harder.

I want to move away to escape the agony, but all I can do is keep screaming, while choking on my tears. When I lose my voice, I just continue to whisper like I'm casting a spell: 'Please stop, you're hurting me, please stop.'

But he smirks in response and continues piercing my asshole until he comes.

He rolls off my back, wiping the sweat off his smug phiz with the sheet. 'She was right. You are a lot of fun, Victoria.'

I get off the bed, still feeling the sharp pain, and quickly pick my clothes up off the floor.

'What do you mean? Who was right?' My voice is quiet and hoarse from screaming.

He gives me a wide smile back, gets up to reach the cigarettes, 'Your pimp. What's her name? Alexandra.' He takes a deep drag. 'She told me you would do anything for a hit.'

The blood floods my head and I feel like I am going to pass out, but I manage to take a few steps and get to the bathroom. I notice a few red drops running down my legs. No kidding. The fucker ruptured me.

It's okay, Jul. It hurts, but will not kill. Calm down and let's get out of here first … you can cry about it later.

I dress while suffocating from tremendous humiliation and pain. When I walk back out to the bedroom I do my best to pretend that nothing happened: I don't want to show the bastard that I am afraid of him – or, worse, make him angry. When he sees me all dressed, he lifts his eyebrows.

'I assume you are not staying overnight, Sweetie? I hope you don't expect me to pay you the full amount.' He enjoys every word with that damn smirk and pushes a hundred bucks into my hand. Then, he heads to the front door and opens it wide. 'I hope you enjoyed it too, Victoria, and that I will see you again.'

Sick motherfucker! I wish I could smash that arrogant smile off your face right now!

But instead I take the money and leave without saying a word.

I quickly walk down the stairs. As soon as I am on the street I start weeping: the fear and humiliation, mixed with the rage of knowing that Alexandra just set me up, make it unbearable for me. I don't know how to handle it.

What a bitch! I am going to trash her ...

48

I jump into the cab and dial Alexandra.

'The fucker raped me!' I scream hoarsely at the cellphone as soon as I hear her sugary 'hello'. 'Is that what you meant when you told him I would do anything for a hit?'

The driver jerks in fright, now checking on me in the rearview mirror. Luckily, we're speaking Russian.

'What are you talking about, Victoria? What happened?'

'He raped my ass, and it's all your fault, you fucking bitch!' I utter, barely audibly, but I don't care – she knows what I am talking about.

'How's it my fault now?' she raises her voice. 'You have sniffed your brains out and became a goner-junkie. Look at yourself in the mirror before you accuse anyone else! Besides ...' she returns to calm and sugary, 'I know this client very well – he wouldn't do anything like that. You probably agreed to it.'

'Fuck you!' I utter out loud.

'Watch your language, Victoria. I am not going to tolerate you talking to me like this. Yes. I knew from day one you were "fine" to fuck without a condom. If the client requested someone with no complications, you were my first choice. No one forced you to be flexible, Victoria. You became that yourself! In fact, you should be grateful that I could give you a lot of work.'

'Grateful?' My throat is dry and itchy and I feel that I am losing my voice again, but I can't stop and my yelling becomes hoarser, 'For what, you fucking bitch, for my bleeding ass right now? Fuck you! Did you hear me? Fuck you!' I say as my voice breaks down. I shut my cellphone and a wave of hot tears starts running down my face.

The driver pulls a bottle of water from nowhere and passes it to me, then gets a box of tissues from the glove compartment.

'*Teşekkürler*,' I thank him, and try to calm down.

As I walk into the apartment, angry Inna is pulling my clothes from the hangers and shelves and throwing them onto the floor, in the middle of the room.

It looks like my day is not going to get better …

'What are you doing, Inna? Are you mad?'

She turns to me and stops for a moment. Her eyes are red with anger and I can see that she is pretty drunk.

'You dirty slut! Aside from turning into a real junkie and bringing your shit to my place, you also sleep with me in one bed, after you fuck without condoms?'

'What are you talking about?' My voice sounds too weak. I have no energy to argue.

'I spoke to Alexandra. She told me everything.' Inna doesn't calm down. 'I want you out of my place! I don't need a crack whore who will bring Aids and God knows what else to my place!'

'No problem, girlfriend, I am out. Will fetch my stuff in a day or two. I will have to find a place to stay first … in the middle of the night.'

* * *

Hi my Poppy-seed!

How are you doing?

I have a hilarious story for you … I bet you will laugh yourself silly ☺!

There was a guy who Natalia trapped last night. As soon as she convinced him to spend some time with her in private, he quickly got drunk and started begging her to have sex. Natalia didn't want to scare him away and wanted to make him buy more champagne, so she chose the storyline that she was madly attracted to him too and would have loved to fuck him right then but didn't have any protection with her. The guy, after three hours and four bottles, got so frustrated that he asked Natalia to wait a moment and ran outside with the words, 'I will find the condoms!' Turned out that at the bus station across the road from the club there was a machine that sold rubbers. But then our boss arrived! He pulled into the club and headed inside as this drunken guy stormed out, bought a few condoms with shaking hands and raced back to Natalia.

She wound up facing two frustrated men and had to be very creative ☺. So she made the guy pay for another two bottles, because he had 'got her in trouble' and 'had to make it up to her' and then after she'd sent the drunk home, she had to listen to an hour-long lecture from the boss (of course, in French again ☺☺!) on how careful she must be, otherwise he could end up in jail on pimping charges.

We laughed half of the morning, just couldn't stop ☺☺. I wish you were with us ...

Okay ☺, I hope it was entertaining enough for you, my little baby. Waiting for your letters.

xxx

49

It's 3 a.m. I hesitate, but dial Ali.

It takes him some time, but I hear his sleepy-surprised voice.

'Hello?'

I start crying. The lump in my throat doesn't let me say a word; I sob pitifully instead.

'Julia? Is that you? What happened? Where are you?' He sounds wide awake now, his voice becoming full of concern.

'I had a fight with Inna.' I can finally voice a few words. 'She threw me out of her place in the middle of the night.'

'Why? What happened?'

'Nothing, actually. She is very drunk again. She was vicious for no reason. I think she already has the jimjams. She even attacked me with a knife!'

I lie. I cannot tell him the truth. And I need to make sure I come across as the good-girl victim, to gain as much sympathy as possible.

'Allah-Allah! Is she crazy? Are you injured?'

'No, I am fine – but I have nowhere to go …' I fall silent and wait, listening to my heartbeat and hoping to hear the right answer.

'Oh … sure, Jul, you can stay with me … Where are you now?'

I sigh with relief and smile into the phone.

'I am actually downstairs… can you please call the concierge to let me in?'

'Damn!' Ali laughs. 'You are quick! How did you know I would invite you?' He sounds genuinely amused.

'Despite your highly developed pragmatism, I always believed that you are an innate philanthropist and would never leave me on the street.' I laugh, while still feeling the wetness on my cheeks.

'Slow down, beautiful', he giggles back. 'It's dangerous for my half-asleep brains to use those puzzling words, especially at 3 a.m.' The sound of him delights, warms and comforts me like a down duvet on a winter's day. 'Come up, Jul. I will make us some coffee.'

50

The next few days are great. While Ali is at varsity, and I am officially fired, I spend the days killing time with some work around the apartment: cleaning, washing and cooking, watching TV, or simply browsing the web and checking my emails ...

I have no idea how long Ali will let me stay in his place or what I should do about my jobless situation, but it feels divine not to be expecting a phone call from Alexandra.

My evenings are dedicated only to one man, with whom I enjoy spending every second. We have fun no matter what we do: watching TV, eating take-aways, or mostly fucking like rabbits.

After a few days of recovery, I finally call Inna to ask when I can stop by to get my stuff. She sounds colder than Antarctica. 'I have a client and am leaving in two hours. If you want to fetch your shit – which, by the way, I have packed already – make sure you get here before four.' These are probably the last words we'll ever speak to each other. An hour later, when I get to her place, she opens the door and pushes my two suitcases out without saying a word, making sure I don't get a chance to walk in.

What a bitch!

On my way back Ali calls. 'How is my beautiful girl doing?'

I love to hear his voice.

'I will be home by eight. Put on something nice and sexy. We are going out for dinner.'

It's a good thing I've got my dresses back. 'Sure, baby,' I murmur and we hang up after exchanging a few noisy kisses through the air.

The place turns out to be a super cool, trendy seafood eatery. We enjoy the meal and each other's company to the fullest, adding to that a few sniffs in the bathroom for aperitif and dessert – which, of course, makes us feel like the world belongs to us.

When the waiter brings the cheque, Ali looks at his wallet and lifts his eyebrows.

'Shit, I forgot I had a fight with my father.' He rolls his eyes and continues, 'You know, nothing serious. The old man is just trying to prove his point and we all know that the only way he can make me listen is to cut me off from the manger.'

He closes the wallet and puts it back into his pants pocket, frowning. 'I hate to ask you, Jul, but could you please get this one? I will pay you back as soon as I've sorted things out with my father ... in a few days max.'

I nod sure and pick up the bill without hesitation.

He leans over the table and kisses me on the lips. 'Thanks, you are the best!'

* * *

Hi my Poppy-seed!

How are you keeping? I haven't heard from you lately. What's going on? I am worried about you big time ☹.

Guess what? I think Natalia is in love! ☺

She met this Russian guy who serves in the French legion. He is a very handsome guy with a great personality and an awesome black Audi TT. He took us on the Gardon River where we had a picnic and did some canoeing. Had great fun.

You know Natalia, she is all cool, and keeps saying that it is not serious, but I think she is totally smitten by this guy, and that he is planning some serious moves on her.

I am so tired – this champagne-drinking for real

is exhausting. We have another two weeks before the end of our contract. Can't wait to go home.

Natalia is making plans already for expanding and improving the salon.

Waiting for your reply …

xxx

51

Fuck.

The next day the same thing happens … and the day after that.

Ali asks me if I want to go out, chooses an expensive place and then bullshits me with his father story when it comes to the bill, adding a stupid-excuse smile when he sees the disapproval on my face.

Every night we go out to luxury places with fancy food and well-trained waiters who remind me of circus animals and who bring me the bill. In return, I get cheesy kisses over the table with a you-are-the-best-I-will-pay-you-back from Ali.

I know that he needs my help. I am sure he will repay me as soon as he fixes his relationship with his parents: but, what the fuck? I worked hard for my money, which now is melting away at an enormous speed to maintain my 'boyfriend's' lifestyle.

Before long, I realise that grocery shopping is my expense and that Ali sometimes goes into my purse, without asking me, when he calls the dealer or goes out with his friends for a drink.

Less than two weeks later, we've pretty much eaten and sniffed up all the money I managed to make during three months of whoredom in Istanbul.

Shit! My sisters are making money and I don't even know what to do? Again, Natalia is swimming in the chocolate with her super-cool Russian boyfriend, while I am wasting my time and my money on some good-fuck-flop, and proving to myself that she was right!

I gently try to point out the problem to Ali, suggesting that now is the best time to get back together with his father. 'Baby, I know your relationship with your folks is not easy, but my money is almost finished and you need to do something about that.'

'Don't worry, Jul. I will sort it out.' He waves me off.

That's it? 'I will sort it out'?

The next day is Friday and Ali comes back from university quite late and already tipsy.

'Beautiful, I am going out with my friends for a couple of drinks. It's Zafer's birthday. Could you lend me two hundred bucks?'

He kicks his shoes off. They fly in different directions. He heads towards the bedroom, probably to get changed. His drunken voice is irritably happy-go-lucky.

'I am sorry, but you know I have only three hundred left and we still have to try to stretch that … until you make up with your father.' I answer loudly so he can hear me from the kitchen and add as much sarcasm as possible to my last sentence, trying to make him understand that I do not buy it anymore.

He comes back to the living room with a bull-like stare. 'Did you just say no to me?'

I am very surprised by the striking change in his mood. Before I say anything, his eyes narrow and he hisses, 'If you are having such money difficulties, maybe you should stop being lazy and go earn some? I could make a few arrangements with my friends … of course, they are students and can't pay you $200, but you will be a smash hit for $50 per night, I promise …'

He is distant and cold. The scorn splashes out like he is a spitting cobra.

'Are you fucking serious?' I am stunned. I can't believe my ears.

'What, Victoria?' He pauses to watch my reaction. 'Is there a problem? In fact, I could call my buddies now and ask if any of them want – tonight, after our little party – to check if I was right about your sucking skills or to nail your little hooker pussy, which, honestly, I am tired of already. That would help us to stretch the money, right?' He relishes every word, filling each one with pure disgust.

'So, are you a pimp now?' I calmly taunt him. I am even more surprised by my self-possession than he is. Usually this kind of shit would hurt me and turn me into a screaming, weeping hysteric.

Oh crap! Don't tell me I am getting used to all the shit that keeps happening to me!

'Why don't you go and let your friends fuck you in your ass instead?' I throw in the same calm way, while heading to the bedroom. 'I believe I've overstayed my welcome here; time to move on. Oh … and I assume there is going to be no repayment, you little swollen-headed prick?'

'Get out of my place, you fucking whore! I am done with you!'

I don't even listen when Ali tags along and jumps into the bedroom, shouting offensive stuff at me. I silently pack my suitcases and leave.

Again.

52

Luckily I left before it was too late.

I still had some money to hire a cab, find a cheap hotel in Aksaray and not worry about living on the street – at least for a couple of days.

Unbelievable! I am in deep shit and still find the positive side of my situation!

I had to make a quick decision about what to do next and the only realistic option that came to me the night I left Ali's apartment was to go back to business as a floozy, but not a call girl. The arrangement is simple: I go out dressed like a normal sexy chick. Then, usually on the dance floor or at the bar, I hook up with a male. For a few drinks I play I-am-horny-

and-I-want-to-be-your-girlfriend with him, making sure that at the moment I tell him about the fees involved if he wants to take it further, he is aroused enough for 'no' not to be an option.

You would be surprised to know how many men feel relief, after slight disappointment, when they find out that the girl they have met is a pro. They don't have to go to too much effort to try to impress me and to get to fuck me. They get a fun evening and guaranteed sex, so they can relax and be themselves.

Inna had told me about the disco bars at which the only girls were *filles de joie*. The male clientele attending them were mostly aware of that, visiting the bars to get laid. The problem was I didn't know where those places were. I had no one to ask. That is why for the last few days I've been hanging out in a dodgy bar next to my dodgy hotel. I managed to convince a few guys to buy my services, but their appearance and financial status were very much below average. I sucked their skanky cocks to earn just enough to pay for the hotel room and to sustain my romance with the stimulants.

I am surprised, but I don't feel too heartbroken about Ali. I am really fine. I guess lately I am always fine as long as I maintain my high.

Obviously, I don't want to admit to myself that my attachment to the powder is now beyond manageable. The tricky part is that I know that I am fucked up already, that I can no longer control myself to stop or at least cut down, even if I wanted to. But nowadays my brain obeys and serves only my addiction. It plays tricks on me – convincing me that I could end it as soon as I make my mind up to do it, and that I continue because I just don't really want to stop yet, making sure that I will supply my body with the next dose in time.

So I didn't even notice the loss of my greatest passion and affection for Ali – simply because my brain decided not to make a big deal out of it so that it didn't distract me from getting my next hit.

53

'Would you like to have some fun?'

I turn towards the voice. There is a short but handsome and well-dressed man standing next to me. *Here we go ... that's exactly what I need right now!*

Without waiting for my answer he orders a vodka Red Bull and 'whatever this pretty lady wants' while pointing at me. Despite me being loaded already, I shout through the loud music, 'The same, but double.'

I am finally in one of those places that Inna was talking about. It's a sizable nightclub, with an up-to-date DJ and stylish interior, promoted over time by its owners from a regular disco bar to a well-known spot for always-available ladies of pleasure.

I light a cigarette and point at the drinks that the bartender, rushed off his feet, has just dropped on the counter in front of us.

'Is that your idea of fun?'

I flirt excessively, lifting my right eyebrow and giving my best hooker smile, making sure that the only message he gets from my body language is 'eminently interested'.

He laughs, throwing his head back. 'Wow, you are fun already!' Then he pulls a sealed little plastic bag, with some champagne-coloured blocks in it.

'Is that what you have in mind?' A wide smile frolics on his face as he teases, shaking the bag then quickly hiding it back in his pocket.

'Now we're talking,' I say quietly and look away at the same time, trying not to give away too much of my excitement to my potential employer. I take a generous sip and turn back to him, putting my hooker-in-action face on again. 'My name is Julia, and yes, I would like to have some fun …'

He throws out his hand for a shake.

'Nice to meet you … Mehmet.' He steps closer without taking his eyes off me, and continues, while gently tossing an intractable lock of my hair from my face. 'I am throwing a little party tonight for my friends, and I am looking for a few beautiful girls like you, Julia.' He smiles smugly, but doesn't sound arrogant at all. 'Two hundred bucks, what do you say?'

I finish my drink showily, take my little shiny black purse off the stool, and lower my voice to lubricity and business at the same time. 'I'm in. Where to?'

We walk out of the club, breezing through the crowd of overdressed and over-painted girls who are rocking the dance floor, moving as seductively as they can.

Poor men! The humane way would be to put a billboard at the entrance, something similar to those black and yellow warning signs with a skull and crossbones, with the heads-up underneath it: Danger! Hunting in progress!

When we reach his black BMW with darkened windows, he opens the back door for me and helps me to drop down onto the seat.

A wave of overpowering fear strikes my insides when I see the other men, two in the front and one on my left. All three of them are silent, with brutish smirks and rudely evaluating stares. My body shakes from the sudden overdose of adrenalin that fills my lungs with the heavy air of danger. Even my slow, intoxicated brain grasps it – it's not going to be a fun ride. I jerk in the hope of getting out of the car but the only exit is blocked when Mehmet possessively gets inside and sneers, 'She is perfect for tonight, a skinny and loaded little whore'.

They all grin. The car takes off.

'Where are we going?' I'm freaking out, but still try to keep my voice untroubled. 'Where are the other girls?'

Before I finish my words the elbow of the one on the left flashes in front of my eyes. The piercing pain from his strike to my face knocks me out.

The rude dragging brings me back to consciousness. The one who'd hit me throws me over his shoulder as if I were some gazelle he'd just wounded while hunting. I try to understand what is going on. I struggle to open my eyes. The first thing I'm able to focus on is the trail of drops of my own blood on the streetlamp-lit paving. The pain and fear surges back, reminding me of what a fuck-up I've got myself into.

Holy crap ... it's sore ... please don't hurt me any more ... please let me go ...

I don't know how long we were on the road, but the quiet, fresh air and noises of the crickets tell me that we are somewhere outside Istanbul, probably in one of the nearby villages.

Please ... please ... please ... somebody ... help me ...

I hear them speak Turkish but the inflamed pulse in my head makes it impossible for me to concentrate and catch what they are talking about.

We walk up a short flight of stairs that probably leads into a dwelling. I am too weak to lift up my head but even hanging upside down I can see the doorframe, the dark corridor, the badly lit room with a couch and chairs. My carrier takes a few more steps and then throws me off his shoulder onto the floor. My head hits the floor; a loud 'Aaargh!' breaks through my lungs, followed by a sprinkle of tears of agony and despair.

The one that was driving approaches me and stands so close that the toe of his shoe touches my face.

'You will have to be a good girl tonight, my darling …' He squats, grabs my hair in a fist, pulls my head up, turning my face to his, and smirks, 'I must tell you I don't like noisy little whores. Although you are lucky to have hit the jackpot tonight, to find out what it feels like when four horny dicks are digging each of your holes at the same time.' The bastard interrupts himself with evil laughter, looking very pleased with his little psycho speech. 'And most likely you will not enjoy it much, but I warn you … keep it quiet and you may stay alive.'

'Hey, Nizam,' Mehmet's voice calls from another room. 'Get in here and have a few drinks with your friends. Leave that whore alone for now. We have the whole night ahead of us.' I hear laughter and the clinks of glasses.

Before he gets up, he squeezes my hair harder, distorting my face to an excruciating grimace while showing me his teeth. 'You will have to be patient, my darling.' He hurls my head back so it hits the floor and knocks me out cold again ...

A splash of cold water onto my face brings me back to consciousness. I return to the horrifying reality very slowly, feeling more and more pain with every second.

'Stay still, Julia.' I recognise Mehmet's voice. It's calm and friendly. He is sitting on the couch with his elbows resting on his knees and looking down at me, 'It's going to be a long and rough night for you, so let me help you to reduce the pain you are about to go through. Besides, it looks like your nose is broken so sniffing is not an option for you right now.'

There is a small black bag in his hands. He unzips it and takes out a syringe with a rubber tube. I shrug away in a weak attempt to object, but the movement only whips up my agony.

He cords my arm and gently injects me, disregarding my faint supplication that's smeared with the blood and tears from my face.

The warm and persistent wave enters my body, as if it's not a two-mil syringe but a bathtub filled with bubbly hot water that's been shot inside me. I close my eyes and drown in a pleasant world, one so generously quick to take over the reality that's poisoned with terror and suffering.

* * *

Hi my Poppy-seed,
What is going on? You are really making me
worry now ☹.
   You don't answer my emails any more. I tried to
call you today too and your cell is off. Please answer
me asap.
   We are back home. So happy to see mom
and papa ☺.
   The only thing that keeps me sleepless is you ☹.
   Please Jul! Let me know what is going on.
Love you a lot.
xxx

54

I come alive, shivering. I am freezing. It is so cold that my numb body is unbearably sore. I am lying on the ground and bright sunlight is hurting my eyes. As I force myself to lift up my head, in extreme pain, I see nothing but miles of tall, dry grass around me.

I look down at myself. My sweater is ripped in a few places. My skinny jeans' fly is not closed. They are not worn properly, hanging below my thighs. There are no panties or shoes at all. I am camouflaged with stains of blood and mud. I don't even want to imagine what my face looks like – it's bloated and covered with curdling blood, which I feel as I wince from the sun's rays.

The memories of last night start flashing through my head, sharp, distressing.

They didn't kill me ... I am alive ...

Despite that I am cold, hungry, injured, and have no idea where I am. I cannot believe I am alive. I don't remember much of what happened after I was shot with crack or heroin, except for some short moments of coming back to consciousness and witnessing every kind of twisted sexual abuse they were coming up with.

The terror, humiliation and pain were all damaging, but the worst experience, it turned out, was the fear of death and then, when the terror exhausted me completely, the comprehension and acceptance of the fact that I was going to die. I guess now I know that there is only one thing that can be worse than death, and that is to wait for it – the absolute certainty that your life is over while you are still breathing.

I start crying, but my body is so dehydrated that there are no tears. As I slowly get off the ground and pull my pants up, I hear the noise. It takes me some time to understand where it comes from. There is a road! And there are cars! I can call for help!

I walk quickly, ignoring the piercing ache that each step brings me. I hug myself, trying to warm up and stop the shivers, which pitilessly worsen the pain.

I wave, but none of the first three passing cars stops. My desperation and self-pity turns my tearless weeping into a wild howl. My vision is blurring, so I feel even more lost and isolated than before. I try to wave more cars down but with no success, until I run into a cop car, which pulls off as soon as the cops see me.

'Ma'am, are you all right?' One of the policemen hurriedly gets out of the car and walks towards me. 'What happened, ma'am? Do you need us to take you to the hospital?'

I want to reply yes, but a weird, persistent rumble plugs my ears and the darkness blinds my eyes, inflating me with unpleasant feeling …

I must have passed out. The next thing I see is an upside down newspaper folded in the back pocket of the front car seat and the sleeve of a police uniform. I am lying on the back seat with my head hanging down off it. I close my eyes again and try to focus on what they are talking about, activating all my brain cells to be able to translate from Turkish.

'Julia Lazar. Year of birth 1983. Ukraine.' The uniform sleeve is reading aloud from the paper in his hand.

'There is no way we are taking her to the hospital. She is just a stoned Ukrainian hooker. Aliens department,' the one in the driver's seat replies.

They had found the copy of my passport in the back pocket of my jeans.

Crap. This cannot keep happening to me.

I sit up and lie back down straight away, fighting the dizziness.

'I need help. I didn't do anything wrong. They hijacked and raped me.'

'Don't even try,' one of them interrupts me, then continues speaking Turkish, with a tiresome tone to his voice. 'First, we do not speak English. Second, we deal with *orospu*[23] like you every day, and I have no desire to listen to your bullshit right now. So shut up.'

An hour later, after being fingerprinted and signing some papers I didn't even understand, I am jailed in a cell with another five women. I know all of them speak Russian, although none of them have said a word. The only two short benches are occupied by four of them, two on each side, and the fifth one is just sitting on the floor, opposite a little smelly loo, which is separated from the cell by a short brick wall.

I go to the free space against the wall, drop myself onto the floor, and close my eyes.

---

23 Turkish, 'whore'

55

I keep waking up. I am in so much pain that even when my exhausted body fades into a short and troubled sleep, my mind doesn't switch off; it keeps throwing me into a mass of agony. On top of my injuries, the withdrawal symptoms are worsening. My skin is dreadfully sensitive and it feels like my blood is boiling, as if I am burning alive.

The hard, cold concrete floor makes my state deteriorate even more. Every time I move my joints, unconsciously seeking relief, it feels like they will crack into pieces.

I am dying ... or I wish I would just die ... that this suffering would end ... not even another second ...

The desperate thoughts of how good it would be if those bastards had killed me while I was still high are fucking me up completely. I can't endure it ... no more ... I need some drugs ... not another second! I can't!

I get up, fighting the severe dizziness, and step to the cell bars. 'Someone, I need help! Please ... I need a doctor!' I shout to nowhere with a hoarse voice.

It's dark and quiet. Probably night-time now.

I hear nothing in response and try again, louder. 'I need a doctor! Help me please!'

'Oh just shut up!' one of my cellmates sluggishly objects. 'No one will come to rescue you, Princess, so stay quiet and let us sleep.'

I step back from the bars, rubbing my arms and shoulders, trying to ease the burning sensation on my skin.

'For how long will they keep us here?' I say to the darkness, towards the voice of the woman.

'Nobody knows,' she responds in the same sleepy manner. 'We stay here until they find a place on the bus or ship to deport us. It could take a day or a week. Is it your first time?'

I don't answer, swallowed up by an extreme desperation. I need a dose and there is no way I can get it here. The withdrawal is getting worse and worse, and I don't know if I can take it anymore.

I go back to my place at the wall, lean against it and slowly slide down to the floor, letting the hot stream of silent tears abundantly wash my face.

I don't know how long I sit there for, staring into the darkness, trying to talk myself through. I force myself to think the only thought that my brain is capable of accepting: that, no matter how painful it is now, it won't go on forever. Until I pass out …

The dry cough that burns my lungs wakes me. My body is shivering. I have a fever. I don't know if it is the withdrawal that's mutated into some kind of cold or flu, or if I'm sick for real from lying on the cold floor for so long. I open my eyes. There is half a slice of white bread on the floor and a bottle of water next to me. I greedily eat it without looking around, ignoring the pain in my face that the chewing is causing, then close my eyes and go back to sleep.

* * *

What is happening Jul?

Are you in trouble?

    I managed to call Inna. She told me a lot of things, but I didn't believe her. She is just a jealous alky!

    I am worried. It has been two weeks since your last email. And your phone is dead! Please reply to me as soon as you can.

We love you very much …

xxx

56

The doorbell rings, interrupting me from finishing my homework, which I've been trying to get out of the way for the last hour already. It's the beginning of May. Summer has come early. It is hot and seductively pleasant outside. But I have a Chemistry test tomorrow and cannot understand a word I am reading in my textbook.

All that seventh-graders can think about is dating and partying. Why can't adults simply understand that and leave dodgy things like physics and chemistry out of our curriculum?

I am alone in the apartment, so I have to get up to open the door. Lena is still at school, my father is working, and mom and Natalia are away in Istanbul.

'Hey, Jul, is Lena home?' It's Serega with his friend.

'No, she is at school still, should be home soon,' I answer, trying to sound cool, but feeling shy: I've been caught in my old home dress by two eleventh-graders, even though one of them is my sister's boyfriend.

'Can we wait inside?' Serega's friend jumps in. I think his name is Pasha.

'Sure. Can I get you some iced water? It's really hot today.' As we walk into the kitchen, Pasha hugs me from behind and jokingly exclaims, 'Uff ... what a pretty sister Lena's got. Maybe I should date you. What do you think, Jul?'

They grin as I try, blushing, to pull my dress back down, which has ridden up from Pasha's unexpected grab.

'What are you up to? Studying?' Serega asks, while winking at his friend. 'You know, Pasha is an outstanding student in our class. He could teach you a lot of things.'

They grin again, looking at each other, and I realise that they are making fun of me.

'Okay, I really have to study. I have a Chemistry test tomorrow.'

'Oh, Chemistry?' Pasha interrupts me and they laugh again. 'That's my favourite.' He moves closer to me and hugs me again, this time from the front, pressing his crotch against me.

I push him away, trying to free myself. 'Okay, guys, you wait here. Lena should be back soon.' I leave the kitchen. But Pasha laughs again, which irritates me, and follows me to the room.

'I can teach you some …'

As we walk in, he grabs me in a tight hug again and starts kissing me, while groping my ass under my skirt. I try to push him away again but this time he forcefully grips my hair, making it very painful for me to move.

'What are you doing? Stop it, you idiot!' I scream.

'Serega, come help me! The doll doesn't want to study!' he shouts while pushing me onto my desk.

'What are you doing? Her sister will come back soon! Are you crazy?' Serega exclaims as he walks in. He knows what is about to happen.

'Tell him … tell him to stop!' I shout now at Serega, while trying to fight with his friend. But as he approaches us he grabs my hands and pulls them down to the desk.

'Let's do it quickly …' I hear, and still cannot believe that it is happening to me …

Pasha closes my mouth with his sweating hand, rips my underwear, then falls on and forcefully penetrates me. I look up with a stare full of pain and pleading, hoping that Serega will take pity on me and stop this nightmare. But it is Alexandra now, who with her animal smile is firmly holding my hands and repeating her sugary 'You really enjoy this, Victoria, right? You really do?'

A stronger wave of pain and terror suffocates me ... the greater the horror in my eyes, the more Pasha gets excited ... all of a sudden my whole world narrows down to drops of sweat that are falling from his chin onto my cheeks ... one after another, echoing his rhythmical, aching strikes ... one after another ...

'Wake up ... wake up ... your sister is here.'

I jerk, trying to understand where I am and what is going on. The dream was so real that I am actually surprised that I am not in my room in Kherson. I've had nightmares about it once in a while, but they'd never been so detailed and close to what had happened to me as this one.

'Jul, oh my God! What happened to you?' I hear the voice that's almost crying, and it takes me a few seconds to recognise it.

It's Natalia!

I get up and walk to the bars.

'Nata ... Nata ... how did you find me?' I start crying as I see the pity and horror in her eyes. I know she is shocked to see me like this. I stretch my arms through the bars and hug her. 'Oh, Nata, you were so right ... it's all my fault ...'

She hugs me back, very firmly. 'Don't cry, my baby sister ... everything is going to be fine ... we are going home.'

Her sobs make her voice quiver.

* * *

THREE MONTHS LATER ...

'Jul? I am busy here with a client. Can you please write down the appointment for this lovely lady?' Natalia is shouting from the men's part of the hair salon.

'With pleasure,' I reply with my welcoming smile to the 'lovely lady' as I walk in.

I've been working in my sisters' salon for two months. Natalia has done some short hairdresser's courses, and now does some of the easier cuts if the three hairstylists who work for them are busy or have a day off.

Lena has learned how to do acrylic and gel nails. It was our mother's idea to expand our services, and since my middle sister set up a table in the women's part of the salon, business has picked up even more.

I've always found touching people's hair freaky, so I deal with supplies and the clients at reception.

I've been clean for three months. As soon as Natalia had got me out of my fucked-up situation she insisted on me going to rehab. I agreed. 'We both know you need it, Jul. It's really difficult to do it on your own. You will have to get proper help if you want to stop,' she told me on the way home from Istanbul. 'Besides, Jul, you look like shit and you don't want mom and papa to see you like this. I found a good rehab a hundred kilometers away from Kherson. Let me take you there.'

I just nodded and we went there straight from the airport. It was not easy, but in the end I came out of that place brainwashed and ready to start a new drug- and alcohol-free life. Now and then I still have my mellow moods and light depressions. It's really not easy, but 'one day at a time', and I do generally feel like a new person.

The most difficult part was coming back to the real world after the month in rehab, when one on one I faced all the evils inside me. My second week 'out' was the worst. My depression put me into such misery that I couldn't even get out of my bed for five days. The only thing that could lull me was a line of coke that I wanted to get, despite the clear understanding that I may not have a second chance to survive. As I was losing it completely, Natalia walked into our bedroom with a cup of hot tea and some astonishing news about my ex-roommate Inna. Apparently she was on one of her regular trips back home on the ship to renew her visa. Obviously wasted, she fell overboard and drowned. It was night-time so the crew only noticed her absence in Kherson port when it was too late even to search for her body. The story was awful, but it encouraged me to stay strong and eventually helped me to climb out of my fucking depression.

It could have been me instead of Inna. It can still be me, if I do not stop moaning and take control of my life … oh, Nata, what would I do without you …

All the way from Istanbul I couldn't stop crying and apologising to Natalia for what I'd said and done. 'You were right. I was irresponsible. I put you girls down and almost killed myself … you were so right, Nata,' I mumbled, wetting the sleeve of her sweater. 'Don't cry, my baby! I never should have said those things to you. No one is perfect and anyone can make mistakes.' She was calming me down, gently stroking my hair. And, after a deep sigh: 'Including me. I've also done a stupid thing.'

I looked at her with worry and surprise.

Nata? A stupid thing?

'What do you mean? What happened?'

'Agh … you know the story about my Russian boyfriend in France …'

'Yes, Lena told me in her emails that he's a perfect guy, and that you two are serious about each other.'

'Yeah, turns out I can be as blind as Lena. He seemed serious about us, and kept telling me. And then I fell pregnant …'

She paused, trying not to cry.

'What? Are you? Now?' I stared at her, pointing at her belly.

'Yes, and the bastard disappeared as soon as he found out about it. He said congratulations, then stopped returning my calls …'

She sighed and looked away. She was ashamed.

'Yeah … so, as you see, I am not Miss Perfect either …'

'What are you going to do?' I asked. 'Are you going to keep the baby?'

She sighed again and said, with desperation in her voice, 'I don't know, Jul. I don't know what I want to do about it ... I haven't figured it out yet ...'

'Oh, Nata, don't worry. Whatever you decide, I am sure it will be the right solution. Besides, you have us to support you, right?'

She hugged me again and I fell silent, trying to process the information she'd thrown at me. I was a little shocked. I would be ready to hear that from Lena, but not my big sister ...

In any case, I really meant what I said; Natalia was good, and would do right in almost any situation. She even handled my troubling situation with imprisonment and upcoming deportation in the smartest way possible. Before getting me out of jail, she called one of her friends she'd known since working in the shipping company. He was an immigration lawyer and had a few connections in the Aliens Department. He made sure that the papers I'd signed before they jailed me, which stated that I agreed that I'd broken immigration law and would leave the country with a deportation mark in my passport, were dismissed, on account of me being a foreigner and their not supplying a translator to make sure I understood what I was signing. The magic touch of his acquaintances also resulted in the police agreeing to free me after Natalia had signed some other papers, showing them our booked return flight tickets to Ukraine.

I understood that hers was not easy decision, but I was sure she would make the right one ... and she did. After a few more days of tearing herself to pieces, with the words, 'I am not going to become a struggling-all-my-life single mom. I will have a child when I am ready emotionally and financially to afford it', she went to a local clinic and had an abortion. The procedure was successful and a few days later she was back in the salon, working her ass off, trying to bury the unpleasant memories of her mistake as deeply as she could.

The business was going well and we were making enough money to keep our family financially stable – and, what's more important, together. The girls even managed to buy a car when they came back from France – an old silver Opel Vectra with an automatic transmission. Both Lena and Natalia had been to driving school a few years ago, but were still too nervous to sit behind the wheel, so most of the time the car remained parked under our apartment building, getting covered with dust. It was a useless purchase, although it made them both feel so much more significant and successful.

Frankly speaking, I have a green-eyed monster that keeps reminding me that I'd also made a fair amount of money in the past year, and that I could also have had a car or some kind of business of my own. But I try to toss it away, reminding myself to be grateful for being alive, and filling my thoughts with admiration for my sisters instead.

* * *

For the last few days, the salon has been overcrowded. It is the end of December and New Year's Eve is two days away. It is eight in the evening. Lena has just finished her last client for today. Instead of going home to relax, she decides to change her hair colour.

'No! Don't even think about it!' I hear Natalia's irritated voice.

Here we are; another family drama is about to happen. Maybe I should wrap it up for today and slip away before these two crazies put me in the middle of it …

'What is your problem? It is my hair and I want to go black!'

I hear the volume picking up drastically between the two.

'Lena, you will regret it. It's no way to treat your depression! Go and shop for new boots or hook up with some guy but leave your beautiful golden hair alone!'

'Jul?' Lena is calling me to help her to deal with Natalia.

Crap! Too late to slip away!

As I walk into the room where my sisters are just getting started, Natalia's cellphone starts to ring.

She picks it up and Lena and I fall silent, letting Natalia speak in peace.

'Hello? Yes. Irina? Hi! Haven't heard from you for such a long time! How are you? Where are you now?'

While she is busy on the phone Lena grabs my hand and pulls me to the little storage area where we keep all the hair and nail products. She pulls out the box that says 'blue-black' and silently lifts her eyebrows, asking me what I think about her choice.

While I am trying to pick the right words so as not to upset her, Natalia walks in.

'That was Irina ...' She pauses, looks at the box in Lena's hand, frowns, but says nothing about it. 'She is in Cape Town ... in South Africa. She got married there and quit working.'

'Oh, good for her!' I exclaim with a grin. 'Where is South Africa?'

'Anyway,' Natalia interrupts, 'now she works as an impresario and is looking for girls to bring there. She says the money is good, and the work is clean. She swears that the strip club is for real ...'

Unfuckingbelievable! She is actually considering it! She was the one who was all, 'Never again!' and 'Look what happened to Jul!' and 'It's so nice to be home together' ... and now there is this sparkle in her eyes! She is actually considering going to this who-the-hell-knows-where-it-is country! No way! Over my dead body ...